Must *This* Show Go On?

Why, why, *why* does it have to be Deena up there? Kathy asked herself. Why couldn't it be anybody else but Miss Prisspot, Know-It-All, Bossy Deena?

"Well, for a first time through," Deena began cheerily, "I'd say it wasn't too bad. But, Lisl . . . How can I put this?" Deena paused for thought. "I don't think the essence of your character has yet been grasped. Lisl *is* innocent, but she is lively and very thrilled about her first crush."

Crush! That was just what Kathy felt like doing to Deena! The "essence of her character"! Kathy really didn't think she was going to be able to take Ms. Deena in her managerial capacity for a whole month. She really didn't.

Cranberry Cousins

A CLASS ACT

BY CHRISTIE WELLS

A Troll Book

Library of Congress Cataloging-in-Publication Data

Wells, Christie.
A class act / by Christie Wells.
p. cm.—(The Cranberry cousins; #3)
Summary: Kathy's unsatisfactory grades and poor attitude lead the guidance counselor to insist she participate in an extracurricular activity, and when Kathy tries out for a school production of "The Sound of Music" she is not pleased to see that cousin Deena is trying for the same part.
ISBN 0-8167-1500-9 (lib. bdg.) ISBN 0-8167-1501-7 (pbk.)
[1. Cousins—Fiction. 2. Plays—Fiction. 3. High schools—Fiction. 4. Schools—Fiction.] I. Title. II. Series: Wells, Christie. Cranberry cousins; #3.
PZ7.W4635Cl 1989
[Fic]—dc19 88-16940

A TROLL BOOK, published by Troll Associates
Mahwah, NJ 07430

Printed in the United States of America.
10 9 8 7 6 5 4 3 2 1

Chapter 1

As her English teacher's dreary voice filled the classroom, Kathy Manelli filled in the heavy black outline of the letter A on her notebook with a hot-pink Day-Glo marker. It certainly brightened up the bleak late February day and looked fantastic next to the wild yellow W. Kathy was doing each letter in NUCLEAR WASTE, her favorite band, in a different, far-out color.

The teacher's voice raised slightly. "Now, who can tell me the significance of the opening scene from *Macbeth*?"

Kathy slouched down in her seat. She tried to disappear, but it wasn't easy in the blazing turquoise sweat shirt she'd chosen that morning because it looked so fabulous with her new black mini and her mustard suede over-the-knee boots. She scooched down another few inches, hoping Mrs. Godfrey wouldn't call on her. She'd meant to do the reading assignment the night before. But when her friend Ellecia had phoned to tell her that Nuclear Waste's entire double album was being played on

WPTB, no commercials . . . well, it had been totally impossible to read and listen at the same time.

From her seat in the back row, Kathy saw her cousin Deena's hand shoot up and wave frantically under Mrs. Godfrey's nose. She watched Mrs. Godfrey get that mushy look on her face, the look she got when she was about to call on a student she knew would give a great answer.

"Deena?" Mrs. Godfrey said.

Deena stood by her desk to answer. Kathy still couldn't get over how she stood up like that in class. Deena had explained that they had been taught to answer this way at her old school in Boston. What made it worse was that some students here at Cranford were starting to stand up when they answered, too, like Deena. Not me, thought Kathy. No way.

"The three witches," Deena was explaining in an excited way, as if she were really interested in *Macbeth*, "are symbolic of evil, and they foreshadow evil events to come. The lines 'Fair is foul, and foul is fair' foreshadow a moral reversal that—"

"Excellent, Deena. Thank you." Kathy could tell Mrs. Godfrey hated to interrupt Deena. "Let's give someone else a chance to answer, too."

Deena sat down.

With her marker Kathy poked Ellecia, who was slumped down in the desk directly in front of her. "Swap me this hot pink for that chemical green, would you?" she whispered.

Ellecia nodded her brown and, this week, bright blue head and handed back her marker. Kathy bent over her notebook to do some serious inking on the letter S. *A subatomic attraction, baby*, Kathy hummed to herself, *like a total reaction, baby*. She never heard the classroom door open or noticed the school secretary come in and hand Mrs. Godfrey a note. The first she knew that something unusual was happening was when Mrs. Godfrey stopped talking for a moment, and then announced, "Kathy Manelli, you are wanted in Mrs. Dietrich's office."

Kathy fumbled her grip on the marker, making a yellowish-green streak down the front of her notebook. She looked up at Mrs. Godfrey and pointed to herself. "Me?" she mouthed, unbelieving. Mrs. Godfrey nodded. "Go ahead and take your books, Kathy. Third period is about over anyway."

Kathy's face was burning. As she shuffled her books into a pile on top of her notebook, Deena caught her eye. Her cousin looked puzzled, Kathy thought, as if she felt sorry for her. Deena quickly held up crossed fingers, wishing Kathy luck.

Heading for the classroom door, Kathy bent her head, trying to hide her face. What could Mrs. Dietrich want with her? What could be serious enough for the guidance counselor to call her out of class?

As she walked slowly down the steps to the faculty offices, Kathy's mind raced. Maybe Mrs. Dietrich found out about the time she cut gym with Ellecia. Why had she let Ellecia talk her into sneaking into the parking lot to pig out on a box of chocolate-covered doughnuts anyway? She didn't even *like* chocolate doughnuts. But that had been weeks ago. And Kathy was pretty sure no one had seen them. Kathy thought harder. She wondered if it was that time she'd fallen asleep in study hall after being up so late watching those Bruce Springsteen videotapes with her boyfriend, Roy. But would sleeping be a serious enough offense to call her out in the middle of class? Maybe it was about the time Mrs. Godfrey had intercepted a note she'd passed to Ellecia. Or one of the many times she'd gotten caught without her homework. Kathy's mind filled with a long list of her crimes. But none of them seemed major *major*. None of them except... algebra! That was it! That had to be it—she was flunking algebra! She was going to get her first big fat F!

Dreading what was to follow, Kathy reached the heavy wooden door that announced in crisp white letters: MRS. ARLENE DIETRICH, GUIDANCE COUNSELOR. Kathy knocked.

"Come in," Mrs. Dietrich called.

Kathy pushed open the door. Mrs. Dietrich was writing something and didn't look up, but Kathy caught sight of a report card with her name on it beside her elbow.

"Sit down, Kathy," Mrs. Dietrich said. "I'll be right with you."

Kathy lowered herself into the green fake leather chair that faced Mrs. Dietrich's desk and nervously pulled at a thread on her skirt. Eyeing Mrs. Dietrich, Kathy thought that *long* was the only word for the guidance counselor. She had a long, thin body, long legs, long feet, and long fingers ending in long, red polished nails. She had a long, narrow face, and her long hair was twisted into a long knot that ran from the top of her head to the base of her neck. Kathy thought that she probably liked to keep her students waiting as long as she could.

"There." Mrs. Dietrich quickly proofread the page she'd been writing and laid it aside on her desk. She gave

Kathy a long look. "Kathy Manelli," she said at last. "I have something to show you." She picked up Kathy's report card and, with her long arm, extended it to Kathy.

"Thank you," Kathy murmured, taking the report card. She opened it slowly, steadying herself to see the F. English, she read, C plus. Biology, B. Art, B minus. Chorus, B plus. Gym, C. History, C. Algebra, C minus. Kathy looked up quickly. C minus wasn't that great, but it wasn't an F. It wasn't even a D. For a moment Kathy wondered if Mrs. Dietrich had called her in to congratulate her on passing everything. "Thank you," Kathy said again, handing the report card back to Mrs. Dietrich.

Mrs. Dietrich sighed. "Your grades aren't that bad this quarter, Kathy, but I have a sheet of comments here," she continued, "from your teachers, and they're the kind of comments, Kathy, that I find most distressing. Listen to this one. It was written by Mrs. Godfrey." Mrs. Dietrich cleared her throat. " 'Kathy rarely reads the assignments before class, yet when she does, she makes valuable contributions to class discussions. If only she would try harder to work up to her potential, Kathy could be a top student.' "

Mrs. Dietrich gave Kathy a withering look. Kathy pulled at the little spiky hairs she'd cut last week just in front of her right ear.

"Here's one from Mr. Millander," Mrs. Dietrich went on. " 'Kathy could do well in American history if she would only shed her apathetic attitude and start trying.' " Another long look from Mrs. D. "Shall I read some more?"

"You don't have to," Kathy said grimly. "I think I know what they'll say."

Mrs. Dietrich nodded. "Every one of them," she said. "Now, I've looked up your records from California, and I find that although some teachers felt you could do better, you maintained a solid B average."

Kathy nodded, remembering her old school and the good old days before her life had been shaken up like a major quake on the Richter scale by moving away. Had it really been just six months ago that she, her little brother, Johnny, and her mother had sold their house in San Francisco and moved to this tiny nowhere town of Cranford, New Hampshire?

Kathy thought back to that Saturday morning last August when she'd brought her mother the mail. In it was a check for a poem her mother had written for a magazine. In between her stints as a waitress, the poem had taken her mother a week to write. The check was for fifteen dollars.

"I've had it!" her mother had exclaimed, waving the check. "I never wanted to risk my karma by writing for money, but this is ridiculous! When your father was alive, poetry writing was one thing, but now I've got to think of a way to make a *living*!"

That night Kathy's mother had called her sister Lydia in Boston and agreed to the scheme that Lydia had been trying to talk her into for months. The sisters had inherited an old, broken-down Victorian inn in New Hampshire that had once belonged to their parents. Lydia believed that if they fixed it up, they could run it again as an inn. Johnny had thought it was a great idea, but what did a nine-year-old kid know about it, anyway? Kathy had tried to talk her mother out of the plan, but it hadn't worked.

And so, here she was, living in the dilapidated Cranberry Inn in a town where there was snow on the ground for eleven months a year, and sharing a third-floor room with her cousin, Deena, who was her absolutely exact opposite. She didn't even like *music*, except for that classical stuff. Back in California, Kathy had had lots of friends who loved music, the way she did when she sang with her band. She'd had friends who liked to have a little fun. Friends who took things easy in the hit-the-books department and it all seemed to work out O.K.

"Kathy," Mrs. Dietrich finally said, "are you still with me?"

Kathy blinked away her daydream and looked back into the eyes of the guidance counselor. "Sorry," she said, "I was just thinking."

"What I *ought* to do," Mrs. Dietrich said, nodding at the comments in her hands, "is call your mother in for a conference and put you on probation." She looked hard at Kathy. "How do you think your mother will react when she reads these comments?"

Kathy shrugged her shoulders. "She won't be too happy," she said. She pressed her lips together and frowned. Worse than not too happy, she thought, she'll be worried about me and afraid that she did the wrong thing by moving us all the way across the country. Kathy knew that her mom was having a hard time herself, what with all the strain and expense of starting up at the inn. Kathy hated to make it even harder for her.

Mrs. Dietrich folded the comment sheet like a letter and held it up in one long hand. "Kathy," she said, "since you're new here, I'm going to give you another chance. I'm going to make you a deal."

Kathy felt a twinge of hope. "A deal?"

"That's right." Mrs. Dietrich nodded. "A deal. You're an intelligent girl, Kathy, too intelligent to let a bad attitude get the best of you. So I'm willing to toss these comments into the wastebasket and give you a month to earn some new comments, some better ones. Fair?"

"Very fair," Kathy repeated, smiling. "Thank you."

"But," added Mrs. Dietrich, "there's more to this deal. I also expect you to do something to show that you care about Cranford High, Kathy. I want you to put your terrific spirit and energy into some of the positive activities we offer here. So the other half of our deal is that you contribute something to Cranford High—the way your cousin Deena does."

Kathy gripped the arms of her chair tightly and tried not to show her reaction to this comparison with her cousin. It made Kathy crazy to be compared to Deena. They were so different, yet they were always being lumped together as the "Cranberry Cousins."

"Deena started school the same time you did in September," Mrs. Dietrich was saying, "and even though she was a new student, she joined right in, giving her all to the school."

That's Deena for you, thought Kathy. Miss School Spirit.

"She's joined the Pep Club, the Student Council, and the French Club." Mrs. Dietrich counted on her long fingers. "She chaired the Toys for Tots drive and helped organize the Ski Club trip.

"Maybe you'd like to try out for the girls' basketball team?" Mrs. Dietrich was suggesting. "Or go out for cheerleading."

Cheerleading? For a moment, Kathy thought of telling Mrs. Dietrich just to stick the teachers' comments in her report card. She could handle her mom's reaction better than she could handle having to become a rah-rah nerd. But it wasn't just her mom anymore. Now she had a bigger family, and she doubted that she'd be able to keep the comments between her and her mom. She'd have to face Aunt Lydia's reaction, too. And Deena's. She could just hear Deena: "Gosh, Kath, that's too bad all your teachers wrote home about your attitude, although what they said *is* true. Want me to tutor you in English?" She couldn't stand that! No, Kathy realized she'd have to do whatever it took not to come home with those comments.

"I'm sure I can find something, Mrs. Dietrich," Kathy said, hoping this interview was about over. For the first time, Kathy actually wanted to be on her way to algebra.

"I'm sure you can, Kathy," said Mrs. Dietrich. She let go of the folded paper, and it fell into the wastebasket under her desk. Then she stood and held out her long arm to shake Kathy's hand.

"Thank you," Kathy murmured for what seemed like at least the twentieth time since she'd come into this office. She shook Mrs. Dietrich's hand and walked quickly to the door.

"And Kathy?" Mrs. Dietrich called as she'd just about made it out of the office.

"Yes?"

"I'll be keeping an eye on you."

Chapter 2

When English class ended, Deena smoothed her kilt and adjusted the navy blue cardigan she had pulled over her shoulders. Then she collected her books. She had been intending to loiter in the hallway after class and just possibly bump into Ken Buckly, who had English next period in the same room. Ken was everything Deena dreamed about in a boy: he was smart, very smart, and he appreciated *good* music. He even played French horn in the school orchestra. Plus he was a junior, president of the Ski Club, and a dynamic athlete. Deena had the feeling that Ken looked forward to their daily meeting at this time as much as she did. But she'd have to give it up today. Family responsibility came first. Now she planned to march straight to the guidance counselor's office. She would wait for Kathy in the hall and make sure everything was all right before she went to her history class. She hoped Kathy wasn't in trouble. But, if there was some problem, well, she'd help Kathy with it. After all, that's what family was for.

As Deena approached the stairs, she saw Margaret

McCabe coming up to the second floor. Deena had become aware of Margaret her first day at Cranford. She had what Deena thought of as star quality. She was tall and stately and beautiful, with long, wavy yellow hair and big brown eyes. Margaret was in the Honor Society and ran just about everything for the senior class. But her real claim to fame was that she always starred in the Cranford High musical productions. Deena had admired her so much in the role of Kim in this fall's production of *Bye Bye Birdie*.

Deena gave Margaret a small smile as she headed down the stairs and couldn't have been more surprised when Margaret stopped and spoke to her.

"You're Deena Scott, aren't you?" Margaret asked in her lovely lilting voice.

"That's right," said Deena.

"You're one of the people I wanted to see," said Margaret, nodding at Deena. "This is really fortunate, bumping into you like this."

Deena's smile broadened. She waited, with thumping heart, to hear why Margaret wanted to see *her*.

"Tryouts for the spring musical are this Thursday," Margaret explained. "And there are so *many* wonderful parts that I wanted to encourage some of you underclassmen to try out. We seniors will be graduating soon, and there's a group of us who want to make sure there's some new blood to carry on our tradition of excellence."

"Sure," said Deena, already planning how she could rearrange her busy schedule to fit in rehearsals. "I'd love to. Theater *is* one of my most passionate interests. 'The play's the thing,' you know."

"Exactly," said Margaret, nodding. "And it's not that

we're snobs or anything, but we—a group of us who have been performing in the shows for three years—we feel we'd like to select whom we wish to carry on in the plays. You understand?"

"Perfectly," said Deena.

Margaret gave Deena's arm a little squeeze. "I knew you would! See you after school on Thursday. In the music room."

Deena watched as Margaret turned and walked down the hall, nodding to the left and to the right, smiling at the other students in a sort of royal way.

Deena had been in plays before, of course. But never a musical. Could she do it? she wondered. She wanted to, she realized, very much. She wanted to be a part of Margaret McCabe's world. Well, she'd try her hardest, that was for sure. But she decided right then and there that she'd keep her tryouts a secret. That way, if she didn't make it, no one would know. And if she did.... She could just picture herself up on that stage singing her heart out. She wondered what musical it was that Cranford was doing this spring. Well, it didn't really matter. What mattered was that she, Deena Scott, might get to play a part!

Consulting her watch, Deena realized that she didn't have time to find Kathy between classes now. As she headed for her history class, she thought that it probably just would have annoyed Kathy anyway to see her waiting outside the guidance counselor's office. Kathy did appreciate her privacy.

Deena walked down the hall toward her class, smiling and nodding to each student she met.

Chapter 3

The three o'clock dismissal bell was still ringing as Kathy charged out the wide front doors of Cranford High. She galloped down the steps and broke into a run on the sidewalk.

"Katheeeee! Wait up!"

Kathy wanted to run faster at the sound of Deena's voice, but she slowed her pace and waited for her cousin. When she reached the street, she stopped and kicked at a glob of soot-blackened snow in the gutter and thought how in San Francisco, in February, the temperature would be in the fifties.

Deena put a hand on Kathy's shoulder and walked beside her, catching her breath in big frosty puffs in the chill air. "What's the big hurry?" she asked finally.

Kathy shrugged. "I've got tons of stuff to do tonight."

"So what happened?" Deena asked. "When you had to go to Mrs. Dietrich's office?"

"Nothing much," answered Kathy as they turned off the sidewalk in front of their school and onto the windy, winding road that led up the hill to the inn.

"But what?" Deena insisted, adjusting her muffler to protect her face better. "I'm dying of curiosity!"

"You know what happened to the cat," muttered Kathy, stalling for time. She couldn't confide her troubles to Deena. Deena would think it was a *great* idea for her to join a bunch of dinky clubs at school. She'd probably want to start making a list of possible activities as soon as they got home. Kathy just didn't want to deal with Deena's go-for-it attitude. "Uh, it was about some test scores," Kathy mumbled at last.

"What test scores?" asked Deena. "We haven't even taken any standardized tests here in Cranford yet. Now, in Boston, we had batteries of tests every year, simply *batteries* of them."

Without meaning to, Deena had given Kathy her story. "Yeah," Kathy began, "well, these were some tests I'd taken in California. They showed I scored real high in, um, English."

"English?" Deena gave Kathy a look like maybe she hadn't bought this story all the way. "What kind of English? Your knowledge of literature? Or your command of grammar? Or sentence structure? Or—"

"Just English," stated Kathy. "The whole ball of wax. Hey, listen," she added, wanting desperately to change the subject, "speaking of English, you know I got a tape of that new group from London, Foggy Heads? But I haven't been able to listen to it yet because my head phones are missing. You haven't seen them, have you?"

Deena shook her head. "Sorry," she said. "Frankly, I don't see how you find anything on your side of the room. Très messay!"

"Très messay," Kathy imitated Deena in a sing-song voice. "Is that what you learn in French Club?"

"Oh, you know what we're doing in French Club?" asked Deena, unfazed by Kathy's remark. "It's the neatest thing! We're going to have a dinner at Chez René and order our meal totally in French and speak French throughout the whole meal!"

"Sounds ooh la la," said Kathy, mimicking a French accent.

"I thought of the idea," Deena admitted, "but everyone in the club voted to do it."

"Hmmm," said Kathy, noticing a huge smudge of soot on her left boot. She guessed that Aunt Lydia had been right when she'd said that yellow suede boots weren't really practical for a New England winter. But still, they were so great looking!

"Hey!" Deena only said *Hey!* like this when she got one of her brainstorms. "Why don't you join French Club, Kath? You take first-year French."

"*Merci*, but no *merci*," said Kathy.

While Deena babbled on about the French Club dinner, Kathy made an important decision: she would find out what activities Deena didn't belong to at Cranford—if there *were* any —and she'd keep her end of Mrs. D's deal by joining one of those.

The cousins reached Cranberry Inn, both winded from walking the steep slope. They both stopped and looked at the massive old house. Sometimes Kathy couldn't really believe she lived there. And even though she missed California in the worst way, she had to admit it was interesting to live in a house with thirteen bedrooms, three towers, four sets of winding staircases—one on the *out-*

side of the house—and six balconies. Johnny was convinced there were secret passages under the house and was always going off to search for them. Kathy loved the room that she and Deena shared, with its ceiling that slanted so low at some points you had to duck to get around and its wide leaded-glass window with the big window seat. If only she didn't have to share it . . . .

As Kathy opened the inn gate, she heard a sound that made her feel happy for the first time that day: the roar of a familiar motorcycle. She turned to see Roy Harris zigzagging up the road. Roy was the single best thing about Kathy's new life. Her mom wasn't wild about the fact that his main mode of transportation was a motorcycle, but ever since he'd helped out at the inn doing odd jobs, her mom and even Aunt Lydia had sort of come around in their attitude toward Roy. He did have a really sweet side that people missed sometimes when they saw his spiked hair and his tiny gold earring. But wait a minute! There was a passenger on the back of Roy's bike, a passenger with a shock of blue hair hanging over one eye. On the seat that Kathy had thought was strictly reserved for her rode Ellecia Spink.

Roy pulled his bike over to the fence and turned off the motor.

"Hey," said Kathy coolly, not looking at Ellecia.

"Hi, Roy! Hi, Ellecia!" said Deena. "Well! I've got so much homework tonight that I want to get started on it right away. See you!" Deena turned and scampered up the sidewalk to the inn.

At least, Kathy thought, Deena knew when to make an exit.

"Pack your bags," Roy told Kathy as he flipped down his kickstand. "We're heading to Niagara Falls tonight. Just the two of us."

"Sorry," Kathy said, still ignoring Ellecia, "I've already got a date to go to Vegas."

"So spill, Kathy," said Ellecia, as clearly as she could considering that the wad of purple gum she was chewing filled her entire right cheek. "What was up with you and Mrs. D. this morning?"

"Just some fuss about test scores," Kathy said, leaning against the inn's picket fence. "No big deal."

Ellecia transferred her gum to her left cheek. "I about wet my pants when you got called out of Godfrey's class like that," she said. "All afternoon I kept thinking, 'Maybe they're gonna send for me next.' "

"I appreciate your concern." Kathy's sarcasm was lost on Ellecia.

"That's O.K.," said Ellecia. "Hey, wanna go over to Sound Systems? Zee told me they got in the new Hot Skin tape."

"Not right now," said Kathy.

"O.K., that's cool," said Ellecia. "I can wait."

Kathy thought quickly. "I told my mom I'd help her peel some apples for the cobbler tonight. Roy, I know you'll help me." Kathy gave Roy a wink. "You want to help, too, Ellecia? Peel a couple dozen apples?"

"Oh, I don't know," said Ellecia. "Maybe some other time." She flattened her gum with her tongue and blew a bubble that popped quickly in the frigid air, coating her upper lip in purple. Spitting the large portion of her gum into her gloved fingers, she daubed it on her face to remove the results of her bubble. Then Ellecia started down the hill. "I'm outta here," she called to them. "Maybe I can still meet up with Zee at Systems. Check you guys later."

Kathy waved to Ellecia as she took Roy's arm and herded him through the inn gate.

"Apples?" Roy was saying. "I don't do apples, Manelli. Windows, maybe. Apples, no way."

"Come on. We don't even have any guests at the moment, so there's no big cobbler emergency," said Kathy. "I just wanted to scare Ellecia off so we could talk for a while."

Roy smiled. "Good thinking."

Kathy led Roy around to the back porch of the inn. She tossed her books onto the porch floor and sat down beside Roy on the big old wooden swing. Its squeaking sound always comforted her somehow.

"Have I ever had a baaaaad day!" Kathy moaned.

"What happened?" he asked. "You had to go see Mrs. Dietrich?"

Kathy nodded. "She called me in and told me to shape up my attitude." She pushed her foot against the floor to keep the swing going. "Or else."

"Or else . . . ?" asked Roy, slicing a finger across his throat.

"Or else . . . bad news," said Kathy, not wanting to go into all the gory details of the teachers' comments.

"Mrs. D.'s tough," said Roy. "Last year she followed me around like a bloodhound to make sure I wasn't cutting classes with some of my friends."

Mrs. Dietrich's words echoed in Kathy's head. *I'll be keeping an eye on you.* Kathy groaned. "She's on my case now," she said. "Like a bloodhound, huh?"

Roy nodded. He looked over at Kathy's face. Her usually easy smile had been replaced by a worried frown. He wished he could make the smile reappear. "I still see her in the halls sometimes," he said dramatically, "hot on my trail." Roy sniffed all around Kathy in imitation bloodhound style.

It worked. Kathy giggled, pushing his face away.

"Hey!" Roy said, sniffing the air again. "I think there is some cobbler in the oven!" He sprang from the porch swing, pulling Kathy off with him. "What do you say we go bury your sorrows in a nice, big helping of hot apple cobbler?" Roy began guiding Kathy toward the kitchen door. "*Vamanos*! *Vamanos*! *Andele*, *muchacha*!"

"*Sí, señor*," answered Kathy, scooping up her books and going through the kitchen door. But halfway in she stopped. "Roy," she said, "do you happen to know if there's a Spanish Club at Cranford?"

Chapter 4

The minute she'd seen the passenger arriving at the inn on the back of Roy's motorcycle, Deena began trying to put as much distance between herself and Ellecia Spink as possible. She just didn't understand how Kathy could possibly like that punked-out Martian.

Deena ran up the wooden steps to the inn, crossed the wide porch, and entered through the front door. The silence inside the inn almost stopped her until she remembered that the last guest had checked out the Sunday before. Ski season was ending. It would be a few weeks until the next guests arrived to view the budding New England spring. Until then the inn was the private domicile—Deena liked this new vocabulary word they'd learned in Mrs. Godfrey's class—of Deena and her mother, her aunt Nancy, Kathy, and her little cousin Johnny.

Deena stopped beside the hall table to check the mail. Two weeks ago she'd joined a new Biography Book Club. Now she was waiting eagerly for her first selection, *The Life of F. Scott Fitzgerald*. She flipped through the letters. Bills, catalogs, more bills. More bills. And there it was! Her book, in a brown cardboard wrapper. Adding it to her already towering pile of books, Deena ran into the kitchen.

"It's here!" she announced breathlessly to her mother, who sat at the big wooden roll-top desk, going over some papers.

"What's here, honey?" Her mother smiled at Deena, her pencil poised in midair.

"The book I ordered on Fitzgerald!" Deena exclaimed as she put her load down on the long oak table. She stepped over Johnny, who was playing some sort of game with red and blue Lego pieces. "Hi, Johnny!" she said cheerfully as she went to the fridge and pulled out a strawberry yogurt for an after-school snack.

"Penalty!" shouted Johnny to no one in particular. He moved a red Lego figure to the center of his game and tossed a little spit ball toward a blue figure.

"You got a basketball game going there?" asked Deena.

"Yep," said Johnny, not looking up. "Reds are winning."

Deena picked up her yogurt in one hand and the Fitzgerald book in the other, stepped over Johnny and his players again, and laid the book on her mother's desk.

"Oh, that does look good," said her mother. "Nancy," she added, centering the single strand of pearls she wore over her cashmere pullover and turning to her sister, who was bent over looking pensively into the oven, "remember when we had that unit on Fitzgerald in tenth grade? I thought Jay Gatsby was the most romantic figure ever. Remember?"

Nancy straightened up, tugging down her black T-shirt over her shape-hugging jeans. "I hope there's enough baking soda in this apple cake," she mused. "It doesn't seem to be rising."

"But what about Fitzgerald, Aunt Nancy?" prompted Deena. "Didn't you think he was absolutely the best writer?"

Nancy looked at Deena. "Not really," she confessed. "I was more into writers with mystical qualities, like William Blake."

Deena watched as her aunt sat back down cross-legged on the floor and peered steadily at her cake through the glass panel in the oven door. Deena couldn't imagine her mother sitting on the floor like that in a million years. Sometimes it was hard to believe that they were sisters.

Deena's mother put down her pencil. "I've got the list finished," she announced.

"A list?" exclaimed Deena. "I thought we'd finished all the fix-its on your list before we opened."

"This is a new list," said Lydia. "Item one: plaster ceiling in the blue bathroom; item two: clean oven; item three: sort out things in storage room; item four: turn storage room into guest room; item five: . . . "

Deena didn't want to stick around to hear any more items. "Well, I've got about six hours of homework," she said cheerfully. She took a last bite of yogurt and tossed her container into the trash. "I'd better get an early start on it or I'll never finish." Taking her books, she skipped up the stairs to her room. On the way, she thought about how she'd planned to read the new Fitzgerald book this week and then ask Ken if he'd like to borrow it. She had a feeling that Ken would feel the same way she did about Fitzgerald.

As Deena entered the large, third-story room she shared with Kathy, her happiness suddenly evaporated. Taking in Kathy's side of their room, she wondered how one single human being could make a mess this enormous. Deena sighed as she went over to Kathy's side of the room and pulled down a knee sock draped over a picture of a female singer dressed entirely in zippers. She tossed it hopelessly onto the general clothes heap at the foot of Kathy's bed and shook her head. It wasn't that she was such a neatness queen herself, but she liked it when things were organized and easy to find. She simply did not understand how Kathy could keep her side of the room this way.

Deena sighed again and then sat down at her own desk. She always began her study periods with a look at her calendar. Today she would study until five, get back to school by five-thirty for her Pep Club meeting, be home again for dinner at seven, and then two more hours of homework after dinner. And she hoped there'd be ten minutes taken up by a phone call from Ken. Last, she always made time to write in her journal before bed. She flipped her calendar to Thursday and wrote in her newest appointment: Tryouts for school play. She only hoped she'd have time to attend rehearsals if she did make it into the play. Well, she'd worry about that later.

Deena closed her calendar and pulled her copy of *Macbeth* to the center of her desk. Finding her place, she decided to put into practice Mrs. Godfrey's theory that Shakespeare wrote his plays to be heard. " 'The king comes here to-night,' " she read aloud in the raspy voice of a messenger. " 'Thou'rt mad to say it,' " she replied in a voice she felt was quite like Lady Macbeth's. Deena was sure that Mrs. Godfrey was right about reading Shakespeare out loud. It *did* make it clearer and so much more vivid!

By the time Kathy opened the door to their room, Deena was well into the play. She was even standing up, pacing and gesturing as she read, to give her voice a fuller expression. " 'Is this a dagger which I see before me, The handle toward my hand?' " Deena cleared her throat. It wasn't easy to get Macbeth's voice deep enough. " 'Come, let me clutch thee.' "

In a spontaneous leap Kathy threw herself at Deena. "Go ahead, baby! Clutch me!" Kathy shouted over Deena's startled shriek.

Deena's face was hot with embarrassment that her cousin had walked in on her at that moment. "Honestly, Kathy!" she huffed when she had recovered a bit. "How *could* you do that to Shakespeare?"

Chapter 5

"Sopr-r-r-ranos!" Ms. Pope, the chorus director trilled. "Posture!"

Even though she was an alto, Kathy sat up straighter. She was on her best behavior today. As she had passed through the halls on the way to first period, she thought she saw Mrs. D. keeping an eye on her. And after class Kathy was pretty sure that she had seen the bloodhound lurking behind a door.

"That's better." Ms. Pope nodded her head of short blond curls. "Now your diaphragms have room to breeeeeath." She pressed her own skinny middle as an example. "Let's run through the melody again. Sopranos only. Watch me. Ready, and!"

Kathy listened attentively. But her mind was still on yesterday's talk with the G. C. She understood pretty clearly what she had to do in school to keep her part of the deal—pay attention in class, do all assignments, participate in class discussions—but she was still puzzled about what she could do to show that she was full of school spirit.

"Let's try that again, sopranos," Ms. Pope instructed.

The chorus class was learning a new song, but it was an old one to Kathy. She had sung it in a school program back in California.

"Fine, sopranos," Ms. Pope said. "Let's try it with the alto section. Eyes on me. Ready, and!"

Now Kathy sang the words of the song as she watched Ms. Pope until, out of the corner of her eye, she caught sight of something pink. She turned and saw that Ellecia, a second soprano, was blowing a huge bubble behind Ms. Pope's back. At this very moment it was spreading past her nose, past her chin. Kathy forgot about sitting up straight. She forgot about singing out. Ellecia's bubble was expanding past her ears, hiding her whole face. She wondered how much bigger it could get. Then suddenly, as Ms. Pope turned in her direction, Ellecia sucked in her breath and the enormous bubble withered and vanished into her mouth.

"Kathy Manelli!"

Kathy jolted back to awareness. Ms. Pope was glaring at her from the front of the room. The whole chorus class was turned around staring at her.

"Yes?" Kathy said, wondering what she could have done now to cause Ms. Pope to be staring at her like that.

"Kathy, do you have any idea where we are on the page?" Ms. Pope asked. Even with her three-inch heels, Ms. Pope wasn't very tall, but her anger made her look gigantic to Kathy.

Kathy quickly scanned the music in front of her. What if Mrs. D. heard about this? It was only second period!

And chorus was her best class! She sure hadn't been able to maintain a good attitude for very long. "Uh, we were on the . . . third line?"

"For your information, we were singing the fourth, fifth, and sixth lines," said Ms. Pope. "And since you seem to have missed singing them with us, I think I'll let you have a chance to sing them by yourself."

"By myself?" Kathy echoed.

"Yes. Find the place, please, Kathy." Ms. Pope waited while Kathy looked at the music. "Ready, and!"

Kathy began singing, softly at first. But as she sang the familiar song, her confidence rose and so did her voice. She looked Ms. Pope right in the eye as she sang the sixth line, giving it her all.

When she finished, Ms. Pope sighed. "Kathy," she said in a voice that was no longer angry, "that was absolutely lovely."

"Thank you." Relief flooded through Kathy. She had saved herself—just barely—from doom and Mrs. Dietrich.

"And Kathy?" said Ms. Pope.

"Yes?"

"I'd like you to see me after class."

Kathy's spirits sank like a ton of sheet music. She nodded to Ms. Pope. For the rest of the class Kathy tried her hardest to sing well, but her heart just wasn't in it.

* * *

"Geez, Kath!" Ellecia snapped her gum as she gathered her books. "I hope Ms. Pope doesn't send you to Mrs. D. again."

Kathy gave Ellecia a limp smile and wished that she

would swallow that wad of gum. If it hadn't been for her and her big bubble!

"Kathy!" Ms. Pope beckoned from beside the piano. "Come over here, please. This will only take a moment."

Ms. Pope sat down on the piano bench. She was so slender that, Kathy thought, half a dozen Ms. Popes could sit side by side on the bench. Kathy sat down next to her, taking up the space of five Ms. Popes.

"I'm very frustrated with you, Kathy," Ms. Pope said.

That makes you and everybody else, thought Kathy.

"You have one of the best voices I've ever had the pleasure of teaching," continued Ms. Pope, "but you don't seem to care about working to develop it."

Kathy stared down at the black and white keys.

"You do like singing, don't you?" asked Ms. Pope.

"Oh, yes!" Kathy looked up at Ms. Pope. "I love singing and music . . . it's just . . . "

"Just what?" asked Ms. Pope, her eyes turning toward the door as the next period students began to straggle in.

"Just . . . I don't know." Kathy sighed. She wished she could rat on Ellecia for blowing those bubbles every time Ms. Pope wasn't looking. It just wasn't fair that Kathy was the one sitting here getting lectured.

"Well," said Ms. Pope, "I don't want to keep you, or you'll be late for your next class. I just wanted to let you know that I think you could do well—very well—if you'd only pay attention." Ms. Pope stood up. "Also, have you thought about trying out for the spring musical?" she added suddenly.

"Oh, the musical." Kathy racked her brain to think what musical Ms. Pope was talking about.

"I'm the faculty sponsor this year, and I'd love to have a voice like yours in the show."

Kathy sprang to her feet. This was it! She could be in the musical! It would solve all her problems at once! Kathy loved to perform. She had sung with a band in California. Here in Cranford she had tried to find a band to sing with—but none of them seemed to work out. But the musical! Mrs. Dietrich could hardly miss *that* kind of contribution to the school. Deena wasn't interested in music. She didn't take chorus. So, no Deena! Perfect!

"Yes!" she practically shouted at the amazed Ms. Pope. "The musical! Yes, I do want to try out!"

"Well!" said Ms. Pope, eyeing Kathy strangely. "Tryouts are here in the chorus room on Thursday, right after school."

"Oh, great! I'll be here!" Kathy had the urge to hug little Ms. Pope. She'd just saved her life!

"You'd better get going," said Ms. Pope, looking amused now. "See you on Thursday."

"O.K.," said Kathy, taking large strides toward the door. "And thanks, Ms. Pope! Thanks!"

Kathy's head spun with joy as she sauntered to her English class. She wondered what musical Cranford was doing this spring. Last year, in California, the spring musical had been *A History of Rock 'n' Roll.* The kids had done the fifties groups—the Big Bopper, Elvis, Buddy Holly—all the way up to heavy metal—Hot Skin and, of course, Nuclear Waste. Hey! Wouldn't it be dynamite if Cranford would do a production based on Nuclear Waste material? Kathy could picture herself, belting out a tune. *A subatomic attraction, baby*!

Kathy mouthed the words. *Like a total reaction, baby!*

Thud!

"Hey! Watch where you're going!"

Kathy didn't see who she'd knocked into. Whoever it was kept on going. All she saw were her books flying out of her arms, and papers whirling every which way down the hall. The bell rang. Great! Now she was late. Quickly she knelt, snatching up her papers and cramming them in between her books. Just as she reached for the last one, a long hand reached down and beat her to it. Kathy looked up into the face of Mrs. Dietrich, who handed her the paper.

"Thank you," Kathy managed, getting to her feet and backing into her English class. "Very much." She gave Mrs. D. a smile then, remembering how she had a plan. Mrs. Dietrich would see that she cared about school. Everything was going to work out fine. Just fine.

Chapter 6

"Next to broccoli," said Lydia on Thursday morning as she filled three cereal bowls with steaming hot cereal, "I think oatmeal is the perfect food."

"Personal foul!" complained Johnny, staring into his bowl. "Hey! I think mine's got a bug in it."

Lydia leaned over Johnny's bowl. She wished Nancy would get up and do breakfast duty a few mornings. "That's not a bug, Johnny," she said, tousling his hair. "It's just the husk of an oat—where the vitamins are."

"Intentional foul," insisted Johnny.

"The oatmeal looks delicious, Mom," Deena said as she sat down and unfolded her napkin.

How could Deena say things like that, Kathy wondered sleepily as she stared at the brownish-gray mass in her bowl.

"Mmmmm," murmured Deena after her first taste. "Oh, by the way, I may be a little late for supper tonight. I've got something after school."

"O.K., hon," said Lydia. "I just hope you won't be too

late. You know I prefer it when we can all eat together. Please try to get home by seven."

Kathy poured some milk on her oatmeal and stirred it. "What day is today anyway?" she asked groggily.

"Thursday," said Deena.

"Thursday?" Kathy looked up. "Oh, I've got something after school today, too, Aunt Lydia," she said. "But I don't think I'll be late."

Lydia turned to Kathy. "Have you joined one of the after-school activities?" she asked.

"Well, I guess I'm going to," Kathy replied.

"What?" asked Deena. "Let's see," she continued before Kathy had a chance to answer, "on Thursday afternoon there's Student Council, Swim Team, Girls' Basketball, Science Club . . . "

Kathy did *not* want to get stuck this morning explaining about tryouts for the musical. She took one gargantuan bite of her oatmeal and called it breakfast. Quickly she carried her bowl to the sink as Deena rattled on about Thursday's activities.

" . . . Bowling Club, Stamp Collectors," Deena was saying, "Future Homemakers of America . . . "

"Bye!" Kathy shouted as she grabbed her books. She gave Johnny a quick kiss. "See you later, alligator!" Then she lunged for the front door.

"In a while, crocodile!" Johnny yelled after her. "See you soon"—he started giggling—"you big baboon!"

"Johnny! Don't laugh with your mouth full!" cautioned Aunt Lydia. But it was too late. The giggles got the best of Johnny, and his oatmeal came flowing down his chin back into his bowl.

Carefully averting her eyes away from Johnny and his

breakfast, Deena carried her empty bowl to the sink. "I'll see you at dinner, Mom," she said. "Good-by, Johnny."

"See ya at two, kangaroo!" answered the still-chortling Johnny. "You know the place, monkey-face!"

* * *

As she walked from her fifth-period class to sixth, Kathy was surprised to see Roy walking toward her down the hall. He had shop sixth period. Why was he on the second floor at this time of day? Kathy wondered.

"Hey, Manelli!" Roy grinned at Kathy and began walking beside her. "Listen, my life as a handyman's paid off quicker than I thought, and all my riches are burning a hole in my old worn-out jacket pocket."

"Yeah?" said Kathy. "Sounds like new jacket time?"

"You got it," said Roy. "And at fifty percent off. How does this sound: black leather bomber jacket, fully lined, with a genuine fake-fur collar?"

"On you, how could it look bad?" Kathy replied, smiling.

"So come with me after school to Boyd's to check it out for yourself, O.K.?" said Roy. "I wouldn't mind a second opinion."

"You got it," said Kathy. "I'll meet you right after . . . Hey, wait a minute. I can't today."

"No?" Roy looked disappointed. "You off to Vegas again?"

Kathy and Roy stopped outside Kathy's American history class. Kathy peeked in and saw that everyone was already seated.

"You're not going to believe this," said Kathy quickly. "It's weird, but I'm trying out for the school play."

"Oh, yeah?" It was the first time Kathy had ever seen a look of real surprise on Roy's face. "An actress, huh?"

"Right." Kathy rolled her eyes. "It's a long story," she said, realizing she and Roy were the only ones in the hall now. "I'll phone you tonight and explain it all."

Roy touched Kathy's hand and ran his finger up her arm in that way that always gave her chills. "Later," he said, and he sprinted down the hall.

* * *

Usually, biology lab went by all too quickly for Deena. But this particular Thursday the lab was dragging. She couldn't wait to get to the spring musical tryouts.

She'd found out from her friend Tracy that the musical was *The Sound of Music*, which had some of her very favorite songs in it. She couldn't get herself to stop daydreaming about it. Instead of the frog in front of her on the dissecting table, Deena was seeing herself in a forest-green dirndl, playing the part of Lisl, Captain von Trapp's eldest daughter. She saw herself dancing about on the stage and singing about favorite things or about being sixteen, going on seventeen. And at the end of the number, the audience would burst into wild applause, standing up, shouting, "Brava!"

Even though Deena loved to read Shakespeare and other plays, she realized that she hadn't been on stage that much. In the fifth grade back in Boston, she had played the part of a peony in a garden of flowers. In seventh grade she played Beth in a scene from *Little Women*, but she had had to die before the end and had missed most of the applause. She thought she'd love having an audience clap for her. Deena wondered if Lisl had any sad songs. Deena couldn't quite remember, but she hoped so.

"O.K.," said Mr. Koprivika, the biology teacher. "Let's get your lab areas cleaned up, and put your lab reports on my desk."

After sponging off her counter and washing her hands, Deena hurried out of biology lab. She wanted to be one of the first ones to the tryouts. That way she could get her turn over with and not be so nervous. She wished now that she'd taken chorus as an elective instead of adding Latin to her schedule. Then she'd have more confidence in her ability to sing in front of an audience. She hoped the rose-and-tan tweed skirt and the matching rose sweater with the little floral pattern around the yoke was the right outfit to wear today. She felt that it was something that Margaret McCabe might wear. She raised a hand to smooth her straight blond hair.

"Hi, Deena!"

Deena turned to see her friend Pat Rogus closing her locker.

"Hi, Pat!" said Deena, waving but continuing on her way toward the music room.

"Hey! Wait a moment!" called Pat, scurrying after her. "I have something I want to ask you. Are you going to audition for the spring musical production?"

Deena stopped. She nodded, smiling. "You, too?"

"Yes," Pat said. "I'm actually feeling somewhat nervous, Deena," she confessed. "I've never done any performing in my life outside of speech class."

"Don't be nervous," advised Deena calmly. "What could happen? You'll be asked to read a few lines from a script, sing a song or two, and that's it."

"I really don't know if I can do it," said Pat as they reached the music room. "But I thought I ought to try because the experience of being in a school production would round out my high school resumé and make me more attractive as a candidate to the first-rate colleges."

"I never thought of it that way," admitted Deena. "I guess it couldn't hurt, could it? And don't you just adore the songs from *The Sound of Music*?" she exclaimed. "I just love the one about sixteen, going on seventeen!"

Deena again pictured herself as Lisl, with her lovely white dress, twirling and singing. Humming a few bars of a tune about raindrops on roses, Deena entered the music room. There she saw a small blond woman she thought must be Ms. Pope, the chorus teacher. She also saw many kids she knew from her classes or by sight because they were Cranford High bigwigs. There was Margaret McCabe, busily talking to Stewart Sharkey, a senior who was known for directing the famous Cranford productions. There was Jennifer Wing and Lauren Richardson, Margaret's best friends. Deena saw Gerard Alverez, Dee Dee Goffstein, and Bud Wilmont, whom she knew from Student Council.

And—Deena drew in a sudden breath—there, across the room, just like the stranger in "Some Enchanted Evening," was Ken Buckly! Deena stared at him until he looked her way and their eyes met. He winked. Deena felt a thrill go through her as she looked at him and thought about how it had felt to ski next to him. That's where she'd really gotten to know Ken, on the ski trip.

She could have kicked herself for encouraging Kathy to go on that trip. For some reason, Ken seemed to develop a big crush on her cousin the minute he saw her, even though she just wasn't his type. For a couple of miserable weeks, Ken and Kathy had even dated. But at last they'd both realized how completely different they were. Then Ken had started coming around to see Deena now and then. So far, it was all sort of "official business." He'd come to talk about Student Council or Ski Club projects. But now that they'd have this play in common and rehearsals several times a week, Deena thought things were definitely looking up. And she hardly dared to think that maybe, just maybe, she'd get the role of Lisl and Kenny would be Rolf! They'd get to sing and dance together, and wasn't there a kissing scene? Deena couldn't quite remember, but she thought there was.

Deena sat down in the first row. She daydreamed about herself and Ken up on stage as Ms. Pope searched around the room. The teacher checked her watch, stood up, and rapped on her piano to bring the group to order. "All right!" she called into the commotion. "Let's get these auditions underway! We're short of time this afternoon, so let's get to work!"

The talking died away and people found seats. Stewart Sharkey said a few words to Ms. Pope, then sat down at the piano bench.

When the room was completely still, Ms. Pope began. "Welcome to the auditions for this spring's musical, *The Sound of Music*. As all of you know, Cranford has a long tradition of producing excellent musicals, and we hope to make this one of the best ever." Once again Deena saw Ms. Pope scan the rows of faces, as though looking for someone. Then she shrugged. "So let's get started. Stewart, you probably have a few words to say to the group."

Stewart stood up. He was tall and rather thin. Deena liked the way his dark brown hair curled thickly over his forehead and the way he looked so intense. But the thing she liked best were his small, circular tortoiseshell glasses. They made him look, well, so terribly intellectual.

"I'd like to thank all of you for coming to my tryouts today," Stewart said. "As you know, I have directed five musicals over the past three years. I am very proud to have been able to contribute so much to Cranford's fine tradition of great musical drama. I expect that this spring's production will be another success and a continuation of this tradition. I look forward to working with many of you—in fact, most of you, since this production calls for such a large cast—and I'm sure you look forward to working with me. Good luck with the auditions."

Stewart sat back down beside Ms. Pope.

Ms. Pope stood and nodded in Bud Wilmont's direction. "Bud, you and Dee Dee may help me pass out the scripts. Everyone, take a few minutes to look over the—"

The door to the music room was flung open and every head turned to look.

Deena couldn't believe her eyes. She blinked, but when she opened her eyes again, the vision still remained. There, standing in the doorway, was her cousin Kathy!

Chapter 7

"Oops!" Kathy put one hand over her mouth as she stood in the doorway and surveyed the room full of people. "Guess I'm a little late," she said, smiling what Deena thought of as her uh-oh smile.

Ms. Pope smiled. "Come right in, Kathy," she said in a friendly tone. "You haven't missed a thing. Why don't you take this seat next to . . . Dee Anna, is it?"

"Deena," Deena corrected.

Kathy's head swiveled in Deena's direction. She stared in disbelief at her cousin, who was staring back at her, as she strode over to the empty seat.

Deena! I should have known! Kathy thought. How could there be an activity at Cranford that Deena wouldn't be involved with?

Kathy quickly glanced at the other kids who had come to tryouts. Most of them were Student Council nerds. And there was that tall blond girl—what was her name? The one who was always smiling and nodding like she thought she was Princess Di or something.

"This *is* a surprise," whispered Deena.

Kathy shrugged. "Surprise, surprise!"

Deena turned back to a paper on her lap, and Kathy saw that everyone else in the room was bent over papers, too. A serious-looking boy with curly brown hair, round tortoiseshell glasses, and a clipboard handed Kathy some sheets of paper. Then he knelt beside her chair.

"As you probably know," he said in a low voice, "I'm Stewart Sharkey." He paused as if to let this vital information sink in. "I'm directing this play."

"Hey, that's cool," said Kathy. "Oh, I'm Kathy Manelli. I'm, uh . . . trying out for this play."

Stewart didn't smile at Kathy's little joke. He began to write her name down on a list.

"Two L's," she said as he wrote.

"Here's the script we're using for tryouts," he told her. "Find a section that's comfortable for you. You'll have a chance to show me what you can do later."

Kathy took the script. "Thanks," she said.

"And . . . " said Stewart, "I need to get you the right sheet music. What part are you trying out for?"

"Uh . . . " Kathy just couldn't admit now that she didn't know what character because she hadn't even bothered to find out what *play* it was! She cleared her throat. "Well," she said, "what's *your* guess?"

Stewart studied Kathy closely for a moment and finally said, "I'd say it's Lisl, right?"

"Right!" she said. "You got it!" She flashed what she considered to be her most dazzling smile, but Stewart remained serious. Where was this guy's sense of fun?

Stewart sorted through his papers. "Wait a second," he said as Ms. Pope called Amanda Anderson up to the piano. "I've got to go get the music for Lisl."

Kathy nodded. She wondered who this "*Lisa*" was anyway. She hoped maybe it was Lisa Lamamba, lead singer of the Vampire Girls' Band. Now *there* was a role she could really throw herself into. A bar of Lisa's hit single "Dead Eyes" went through Kathy's mind. *Don't you give me that dead-eye stare! Bop, bop, bop, BOP! You know you got the look that I just can't bear! Bop, bop—*

"I have it." Stewart was back beside her chair, handing her some music.

"Thanks," she said. She looked at the title of the song. "I Am Sixteen." Kathy froze, and a bad feeling began rising inside her like thermometer mercury in a heat wave. This song wasn't from the Vampire Girls' band! There, in little bitty letters under the name of the song it said, "From *The Sound of Music*."

Kathy felt dizzy. *The Sound of Music*? She remembered watching the movie on TV when she was about five. It seemed to her she remembered it being about a nun! That's right! A nun who quit being a nun . . . and went around singing with a bunch of children—children dressed in clothes made from sickening green draperies! Wait a minute! There must be some mistake!

Where was Stewart Sharkey? She'd just hand him back the music, hand him back the script, and split!

Deena peered at the music in Kathy's lap. She held up her copy of "I Am Sixteen" to show Kathy. "Same song," she said. "Looks like we're both going out for Lisl."

"Lis-al?" Kathy looked confused.

"Lis*l*." Deena spelled the name for Kathy. "It's an Austrian name." Deena paused. "You *do* know that Lisl is Captain von Trapp's eldest daughter, don't you?"

Oh, no! thought Kathy. One of the children in the curtains!

"There's got to be some big mistake," Kathy said, still looking around for Stewart. She didn't see him anywhere, but she saw Ms. Pope at the piano.

"Ms. Pope," Kathy began, "I—"

"Ah, Kathy!" Ms. Pope beamed at her. "I'm *so* glad you made it today. This is going to be a wonderful experience for you, just wonderful!"

"Welllllll," Kathy began. "I'm not sure I can—"

"You've just got the jitters," Ms. Pope interrupted. "I can always tell. Listen, you go next. That's the best thing to do when you're nervous, just get it over with. What song are you doing? 'Sixteen'?"

"Uh, it's the wrong song," Kathy thrust her music at Ms. Pope. "Isn't there something else . . . another part?"

Ms. Pope shuffled through some music. "Stewart does the casting, you know, so it may not matter what song you do. Ah, here it is." She handed Kathy several sheets. Then she whispered to Rachel Laplant, who was sitting at the piano. "Kathy's doing 'So Long, Farewell.' "

Oh, if only I were leaving! Kathy thought. So long, farewell to these tryouts!

Rachel struck up the intro.

Afterward Kathy could never quite remember singing the song. All she could remember was the happy look on Ms. Pope's little face and Rachel Laplant pounding away on the ivories. In a while, she thought, she must have stopped singing, because Ms. Pope started clapping. So did some of the other kids. Kathy felt red in the face as she went back and sat down next to Deena.

"You were terrific!" Deena said, sounding sincere.

"Oh, I don't know," said Kathy, still flustered. "It's not really my kind of–"

"Really," Deena interrupted. "Just terrific."

"Next," Ms. Pope announced, "will be Jennifer Wing, singing, 'Doe, a Deer.' "

Kathy filled in the letter T on her notebook cover with an orange marker as she listened to Jennifer hit the high notes of her song just slightly off key. Probably no one else noticed it, but Kathy had an ear. That's what her father had always said. "You've got some ear, Kitsy!" he'd say. "A one hundred percent reliable ear." Kathy *could* tell if someone missed a note, even by just a hair. And Jennifer was missing. Not by much, but missing.

"That was fine, Jennifer," said Ms. Pope. "Lauren? You're next."

Kathy colored in her letters as she listened to Lauren Richardson (wobbly), Kristen Bopp (wounded animal), Bud Wilmont (sincere), Ken Buckly (boooooring), Dee Dee Goffstein (sweet), Justin Potter (flat as a pancake), Pat Rogus (nervous Nellie), Gerald Alverez (macho man), and Margaret McCabe (breathy). By the time it came around to Deena's turn, Kathy'd finished the letter E, with electric blue, and was outlining the words NUCLEAR WASTE in "contamination green."

"I will be singing 'I Am Sixteen,' " Deena announced to Ms. Pope and Rachel Laplant.

As Deena began her song, Kathy stopped outlining. She looked up, amazed. Surely she'd heard Deena sing before, hadn't she? Maybe only when she was singing along to something on the radio or the stereo. She tried to remember. Hadn't she and Deena sung a few choruses of "Found a Peanut" when they were painting one of the bedrooms together in the inn? Kathy listened as Deena's mouth opened and closed, and her Adam's apple bobbed up and down in her throat. Incredible as it seemed, somehow, some way, Kathy had never noticed Deena's voice before. Deena, her own cousin . . . Deena, her own flesh-and-blood relative . . . Deena couldn't carry a tune in a bucket!

"That's fine, Deena, dear," Ms. Pope said absently, checking something on Stewart's clipboard against a notation on her own. Deena looked slightly startled, since she had hardly gotten through the first two lines of her song. "We are running *desperately* short of time," Ms. Pope explained, "and we're going to have to shorten things up a bit. We still have the readings to go through." She stopped to write on her clipboard. Then she said, "Deena, why don't you begin the read-through?"

Deena nodded. She wasn't all that disappointed that her song had been cut short. She would rather spend her audition time doing the thing that she did best of all: reading aloud. She found the place in her script, looked up directly into Ken Buckly's eyes, and began.

Even Kathy had to admit Deena could really make words on a page come alive. When Deena again sat back down beside her, Kathy didn't have to comment on her singing but could honestly say, "Hey! that was awesome reading, Deena. Really totally excellent."

Chapter 8

It was after six-thirty when Stewart Sharkey thanked everyone for coming to the audition.

"I will be making my casting decisions tonight," he announced. "This is an area I have great expertise in, so you can be sure that if I assign you the part, it is the right one for you."

What rock did this guy crawl out from under? Kathy wondered. Not only was he totally humorless, but conceited beyond belief.

"I will post the cast list," Stewart continued, "on the bulletin board by the cafeteria tomorrow at noon. If your name is on it, you will need to come back here to the chorus room after school tomorrow for a brief rundown from me on the extremely tight four-week rehearsal schedule. That's it for tonight."

Kathy shook her head to clear it of Stewart Sharkey's speech. Man, he acts like he thinks he's some world-class Broadway director or something, she thought.

Kathy saw Deena walking up the stairs from the chorus room just ahead of her. "Hey!" she called. "Wait up. I'll walk home with you."

Deena turned and waited.

"Whew! How about that Stewart Sharkey?" Kathy asked as they exited from the side door of the school.

"He *is* kind of cute," said Deena.

"Cute?" Kathy couldn't believe her ears.

"Well, you know," Deena attempted to explain, "in a sort of intellectual way."

Kathy decided not to pursue this subject. The cousins walked toward the inn in silence. Kathy chewed on the end of a piece of hair. She was glad that her friends back in San Francisco weren't around to see her going out for this dippy play. She wondered if she could really take going to rehearsals for four whole weeks. And going to rehearsals with Deena! She could just picture her cousin wanting to coach her on her lines every night before bed. Dismally, she wondered what part she'd get stuck with. Because from the look on Ms. Pope's face when she finished singing, she was pretty sure she'd got *some* part. The whole thing was so miserable. If she got into the play, there'd be rehearsals practically every day after school. So when was she going to get to see her friends, anyway? And if she didn't make it, *then* what was she going to do to fulfill Mrs. D.'s deal? What a mess.

As she walked along, Deena bit the inside of her lips and thought hard about the tryouts. It *was* distressing that they'd run out of time just as she was doing her song. She just hoped that Ms. Pope had heard enough to know that she would make the perfect Lisl. At least she'd gotten to start off the script reading. She did, she had to confess, have a way with expressing the written word. She thought she'd given Lisl's feeling just exactly the right expression, a mixture of . . . Deena searched her vocabulary for the appropriate words . . . candor and defiance.

Deena glanced at her cousin as they walked. She did think Kathy had sung her song really well, if you liked that kind of rock'n'roll overtone in "So Long, Farewell," which she, personally, did not. Deena still found it odd that Kathy had even come to tryouts for *The Sound of Music* in the first place. It just wasn't her kind of thing.

Kathy returned Deena's glance and for an instant wondered if she should level with her cousin about her reasons for doing this play. If they were going to be stuck in this thing together, maybe it would help if Deena knew what was going on with her. Kathy sighed. She wished she could confide her secret "deal" to Deena. But, no, Deena would see it as her mission to "help." And Kathy just couldn't handle that. Deena gave new meaning to the expression "Killing a person with kindness."

"Don't you just love this play?" Deena said, breaking into Kathy's thoughts. "It has all the elements of a classic drama. The forces of evil, as represented by the Nazis, battling against the forces of good, represented by Maria and the other Sisters, the—"

"It's cosmic all right," Kathy cut in as Deena nearly knocked her in the side of the head with a hand gesture meant to represent the forces of good. "I just wish the songs had a little more *uumph* to them, like, you know . . ." Kathy moon-walked through the inn gate and up the sidewalk doing her Robots-in-Sin imitation: "Girls with sequin hair. Don't stare! Boys with eyes that glare. Don't care!"

Deena rolled her eyes as she flounced up the steps. At

this moment she truly wondered what the great theatrical tradition of Cranford High was coming to!

***

The Cranberry Cousins entered the inn through the front door. And as they were hanging their coats on the bentwood coatrack beside the front door, their eyes met. Their voices blended in unison as they shouted, "I smell Chinese food!"

They ran into the kitchen and found the rest of their family sitting down at the long oak table dotted with at least a dozen little white cardboard containers.

"Far out, isn't it?" Nancy grinned. "I had to drive fifteen miles round trip for this meal. Dig in! There's wonton soup, spareribs, ten-ingredient fried rice, ginger-showered chicken, and dry sautéed string beans."

Lydia passed Deena the carton of fried rice. "I think we were all ready for a change from New England boiled dinners. And Nancy and I were certainly ready for a break from the cooking."

"Two points!" declared Johnny, holding up a gnawed sparerib. "Let's turn this place into a Chinese restaurant!"

"Maybe next season," said Lydia, looking at her watch. "Eat up, everyone. We have to interview several people tonight for the waitress jobs we posted in the paper."

Kathy dug in, grateful that the play tryouts were not the topic of this dinner's conversation.

After dinner Lydia pleaded with Kathy and Deena to begin clearing out the storage room. "Just tag the items you think should go to Goodwill with these pink tags." She pressed a stack of tags into Kathy's hand. "We'll save the rest. We really need to get that little room ready for guests in just a couple weeks."

Reluctantly Kathy and Deena climbed the stairs and entered the little room just down the hall from their bedroom on the third floor. Deena pulled the cord to turn on the bare bulb in the center of the ceiling. Although it was piled with mountains of old furniture, carpets, and junk, it was a charming room, semicircular, with windows all around.

"Whew!" Kathy said. "It's stuffy in here."

"Really," said Deena, stepping over an ancient headboard to open one of the windows.

The girls began their sorting.

"How'd you end up singing 'So Long, Farewell'?" Deena asked as she shoved an old bookcase to the side of the room. "I thought you were doing Lisl's song."

"I wasn't trying out for Lisl," Kathy said, sticking a pink tag on an ancient wooden file cabinet. "It was a mistake. Besides," she added, "that's the part you wanted."

"Yes," said Deena dreamily. "I really am hoping for the part of Lisl. She's so romantic . . . "

"Hey, Deena!" Johnny interrupted. He stood at the door holding one hand over the speaker end of the new cordless phone. "Phone's for you, but your mom says to keep working while you talk."

Deena mouthed "thanks" to Johnny, brushed her hair out of her face, and took the phone.

"Oh, hi, Ken!" she said softly as she turned an old bentwood rocker right side up and sat down in it. "No, no, I'm not busy. Just straightening out a few things.

What are you up to? You did? At the Video Shack? I didn't know you were interested in that daredevil stuff. Really? Sure, of course I'd love to see it. Well, no, tonight's out. How about tomorrow night? Seven-thirty? O.K. Great! Well, I'd better go. Thanks for calling. Bye!"

Deena pressed the off button and set the phone down. "Ken's got a new ski video." Deena's happiness at having made a date with Ken bubbled over. "It's hot dog tricks. He's bringing it over tomorrow night."

"That's great," said Kathy, remembering that her first date with Ken had been watching a ski video. Originality was not his strong point.

Deena went to work double time. "What about this rug?" she asked, lifting the corner of an old blue and green Oriental.

"Pitch it," Kathy said. "How about this dresser? It's kind of worm-eaten, but maybe it could be fixed up."

"It's not bad" said Deena, running her finger over the old wood. "But I'll bet it's full of moths. Out." She slapped a pink tag on it.

When the phone rang a second time, Deena had to scramble under several layers of carpet and an old bath mat to pick it up.

"Hello. Oh, hi, Roy. Yes, she's here. Just a minute."

Grateful for a minute off, Kathy took the phone. "Hey," she said softly, plopping herself down on the floor. "Oh, basically it stunk. But I'm going through with it. But enough of that. How was Boyd's? I can't wait to see you in your jacket. *What?* Why didn't you? Well, if you liked it that much, I'm sure I would have liked it! I can't believe you . . . Oh, one more chance? Gee, thanks! O.K., O.K. Tomorrow after school. I swear!"

Kathy looked up at Deena. She was shaking her head like mad. "I gotta go," Kathy told Roy. She looked again quizzically at Deena. "O.K., meet me by my locker after school tomorrow. Right. I promise. Great! Bye!"

Kathy pressed the off button, still staring at Deena.

Deena let her hands fall to her sides. "I didn't mean to eavesdrop," she said, "but you know what Stewart Sharkey said about tomorrow afternoon if we're in the cast . . ."

Kathy gave her forehead a smack with her open hand. "So *that's* what you were trying to tell me!" she wailed. "I thought you just wanted me to help you with something!"

For the next half hour Kathy felt like a robot looking at furniture, sticking tags on it, and moving right along to the next piece. Her mind was racing to try to figure out how she should handle this thing with Roy. He always made a big thing out of promises. Should she call him back now and explain? Or just hope she wouldn't make the play? Somehow, she thought, as they slapped a pink tag on an oak fern stand, she just *had* to make Roy understand.

Chapter 9

"Now, who can name," began Mrs. Godfrey in English class the next day, "some of the ingredients that the three witches in *Macbeth* used in their bubbling cauldron when they were casting a spell?"

Kathy straightened in her seat. Her hand went up. She knew this one! Her Cliffs Notes had just hinted at some of the gory things that the witches had dumped into their brew, but Kathy had found it interesting enough to look in the real *Macbeth* and see what it said. It had proved pretty fascinating, for an English assignment.

"Kathy?" Mrs. Godfrey looked so pleased that she was volunteering that Kathy had to stifle a giggle.

"Well, they put in a toad," she said, "some kind of poison toad that had been sleeping under a rock. And they put in a snake soufflé—no, wait, snake fillet! And a frog's toe, and a dog's tongue." Kathy paused to think. "Is that enough?" she asked.

Mrs. Godfrey chuckled. "That's fine, Kathy. I believe

you were referring to the second witch's speech: 'Fillet of a fenny snake, In the cauldron boil and bake; Eye of newt and toe of frog, Wool of bat and tongue of dog.' "

Kathy listened as Mrs. Godfrey recited from *Macbeth*. It was pretty gruesome stuff, all right. Before she realized it, she had her hand up again. "Mrs. Godfrey?"

"Yes, Kathy?"

"Well, you know the metal group Midnight Hags?"

"I don't believe I do, Kathy." Mrs. Godfrey looked puzzled.

"They're an excellent group," Kathy explained. "Anyway, when I was reading last night, I found out where they got their name—at least, maybe they did. That's what that Macbeth guy calls the witches—Midnight Hags!" Kathy could just envision the kind of note Mrs. Godfrey would write home about her now! "Not only does Kathy participate in class discussions, but she also relates her reading of Shakespeare to her own vast knowledge of contemporary music."

Mrs. Godfrey still looked slightly puzzled.

Sometimes Deena just couldn't believe the things that came out of Kathy's mouth. "That Macbeth guy!" But at least Kathy was trying to make a legitimate point, Deena thought. She just needed a little help because, obviously, Mrs. Godfrey wasn't getting it.

"I think I understand what Kathy means to say," Deena's voice piped up. "Her point is that Shakespeare is a great source for things like book titles and, I guess, rock groups. The name Midnight Hags takes on an added dimension from its association with the three witches from Macbeth."

"Yes!" Mrs. Godfrey's face seemed to quiver with joy as Deena spoke. "An excellent point, Deena . . . and Kathy. Excellent!"

Deena looked over to smile at Kathy. But by this time Kathy had slouched back down in her seat and was uncapping a purple-passion marker. Man, how could Deena do it? she wondered. How could she take something gory and interesting, like dogs' tongues and frogs' toes, and turn it into something that no one in their right mind, except Mrs. Godfrey—could ever understand?

As the rest of the discussion took place, Kathy added the hot new shade of purple to her notebook.

* * *

After her algebra class, Kathy shuffled her papers together and headed for the door. As she approached, she noticed that someone was waiting outside. She stopped. Was it Mrs. D.? Trying to assume a studious look, Kathy exited from the classroom. When she looked up, she saw that the figure was only Deena.

"You know, that was fascinating, what you brought up in English," Deena said.

"Yeah," Kathy said. "That gory stuff was kind of interesting."

"No, I mean about the way people borrow from Shakespeare for titles and things," Deena said. "Wouldn't it be interesting to start a list of all the things we know that have their title source in a Shakespeare play?" Deena beamed enthusiastically at Kathy. As they walked down the hall side by side, Deena added, "I thought we could go see the list together."

"You're actually making this list?" asked Kathy, amazed.

"The *cast* list," Deena said with exaggerated patience. "Stewart said he'd post it right before lunch, remember?"

"Slipped my mind," said Kathy. "I'd really rather eat first. I'm starving."

"It'll just take a second," Deena assured her. "Come on."

The girls walked in the direction of the cafeteria. Ellecia caught up with them just as they reached the steps.

"Hey, Kath," Ellecia said. "Think ol' Bill thought up the name for Nuclear Waste, too?"

"Yeah, right," said Kathy.

"Bill?" asked Deena. "Who's Bill?"

"You know," said Ellecia, giving her gum a good pop. "Billy-boy Shakespeare."

Deena closed her eyes for a brief moment. She didn't need this right now. She really didn't.

The three of them walked toward the cafeteria in near silence, except for the occasional snapping of Ellecia's gum.

When they reached the entrance to the cafeteria, there was already a small crowd gathered around the bulletin board.

"Oh, gosh!" Deena breathed. "I can't see a thing!" She began hopping up, trying to peer over heads and shoulders of other interested auditionees.

Kathy hung back, leaning on the opposite wall, her arms folded across her chest. She dreaded what she might find on that bulletin board. Watching the group of eager students mobbed around the list, Kathy felt so different, so removed from them; like a visitor from another planet. Like a visitor from California.

"Kathy!" Deena called. "Come over here and look at this list, will you? I can't get close enough."

Kathy pushed herself off the wall and walked slowly toward the bulletin board. Without much trouble, she made it to the front of the pack. *Maria*, she read, *Margaret McCabe*. No big surprise. *Captain von Trapp—Gerard Alverez. Rolf—Ken Buckly. Lisl—Kathy Manelli.* Kathy read no further. She closed her eyes, taking a deep breath. It was just as bad as she had imagined it might be. No, *worse*! What was Deena going to say? Not only had she gotten the part Deena wanted so badly, but now she'd have to play romantic scenes opposite Ken!

Oh, why Ken Buckly? Kathy hadn't forgotten those few dates she and Ken had had in the fall. He *was* pretty hot looking, if only he weren't so stiff and preppie. Their dates had only proved how different they were, and Kathy hadn't known at the time that Deena had a giant crush on him. Once Ken and Kathy had agreed to call it quits, Ken and Deena had started seeing each other. Things between them were just getting started, and now this had to happen!

Kathy opened her eyes again and scanned down the list. She didn't see Deena's name anywhere! Kathy felt like ripping the paper from the bulletin board and tearing it to bits. She turned to find Deena and saw her talking to Stewart Sharkey. Deena was all smiles. Kathy guessed that she didn't know yet. She hoped Stewart would break the news to her. Then she wouldn't have to do it.

Kathy walked over to them slowly.

"I am glad," Stewart was saying. "I was hoping you'd see it my way. I'll see you at three-fifteen." He walked away from them into the cafeteria.

Deena shook her head slightly. "Well, *that's* a surprise."

"Yeah," said Kathy grimly. "What a surprise."

"It *will* be a different experience from what I was expecting," said Deena as the cousins entered the cafeteria and got in line. "But I think Stewart has made the right choice; my strongest talents do lie in this direction."

Kathy picked up a tray and handed one to Deena. "Which talents are we talking about here?" she asked as she pulled a burrito onto her tray.

"Managerial," Deena said, selecting a fruit salad. "As assistant director, I'll be able to have a wider influence and more control over the production as a whole than I would have simply playing one part." Deena plucked a carton of milk out of the ice chips.

"Assistant director?" Kathy put a slice of apple pie next to her burrito. "Hey, that's great!" She added a bowl of chocolate pudding. "So you're not . . . upset that I'm playing Lisl?"

"Upset?" Deena's laugh tinkled like the change the cashier was plunking into her outstretched hand. "I see my role as vastly more important now."

Kathy fumbled in the pocket on the leg of her jeans for her lunch money. "Vastly," she echoed absently. "And that Ken is playing—"

"Rolf?" Deena finished. "I hope that I'm mature enough to have a professional attitude about this, Kathy."

Deena carried her tray toward an empty table. Kathy followed. The girls sat down opposite each other. Just as Deena unfolded her napkin, Ellecia Spink slid her tray next to Kathy's.

"Thought I lost you," she told Kathy. "Here, Harry," she spoke now to the silver skull ring she wore on her right thumb, "have some fun while I dig into my lunch." She deposited her wad of green gum atop the ring and turned back to Kathy. "Hey, I didn't see that chocolate pudding."

Deena refolded her napkin. "I think I see Ken sitting by himself," she said, standing and picking up her tray. "He's looking awfully lonesome, so if you don't mind, I think I'll join him."

"Don't mind a bit," Ellecia said, spooning in a mouthful of Kathy's pudding. "Ta-ta!"

"See you, Deena," Kathy said, giving her cousin a half-hearted wave. "And congratulations on the directing."

Kathy looked back at her lunch. Ellecia was now working on her apple pie. Kathy felt exhausted from the morning and didn't really feel ready to answer the barrage of questions about the play that her blue-haired, pudding-swiping friend was getting set to ask.

Chapter 10

"Please wait, Roy! It's only gonna take about fifteen minutes. Please!" Kathy leaned on the handlebars of Roy's bike in the school parking lot. "Boyd's will still be open. That director guy, Stewart, just wants to get us together for a couple of minutes and, you know, go over some stuff about rehearsals."

Roy sighed. "Maybe the store'll still be open, but look at that sky, Manelli. Not a cloud. Temperature is like a fall day right here in the middle of February. But by the time you get out of that meeting, the sun'll be going down and the day will be lost!"

Kathy hung her head. She shrugged. "I gotta go," she said glumly. "If you're here after, we'll go for a ride. If you're not . . . " She trailed off as she turned and headed back into school. She heard Roy let out a breath of air and the sound of a sneaker kicking a curb as she opened the door and started down the hall.

"Congratulations one and all!" Ms. Pope was beaming at twenty-nine students sitting in the chorus chairs.

Stewart stood beside her. Deena thought he looked absolutely dreamy today in his beige cords and light blue shirt. She admired the serious quality he had, like a real Broadway play director, she imagined. And those round glasses! He looked so smart. Deena was thrilled by the idea of working with Stewart. "I asked you to come here for a few minutes today," he began, "so that we could go over the rehearsal schedule I have worked out. It's going to be a tight one, since we've got just four weeks from tomorrow before we open. I want to rehearse on Monday, Wednesday, and Friday afternoons from three-fifteen until six for the first two weeks, and for the last two weeks, we'll rehearse Monday through Friday."

Good-by life, thought Kathy.

Stewart held up his script. "There's a script for each one of you on the table by the door. Take one as you leave today, and get a good start on learning your lines this weekend. Then when we meet on Monday, we can really get going. Let's see. Is that all I had to tell you? Oh, this year I have chosen an assistant director to help me with all the work. Deena Scott." He turned to Deena. "You have anything to tell the cast?"

Deena stood beside Stewart. "It occurred to me," she said, "that it might make your memorization process easier if you go through your script with a marker and highlight your part in one color and then go back with another color and highlight your cue, which is the sentence right before each of your lines." Deena looked around the room. "Any questions?"

No one had any questions. Deena sat down.

"We'll go through the songs on Monday," said Stewart, "so concentrate on your lines this weekend . . . ."

Kathy heard the engine of a motorcycle start up, loud and clear, outside the chorus room window and then zoom away.

"I think that's about it," Stewart was saying. "See you on Monday."

Kathy dragged herself out of her seat and started for the door. She thought about waiting for Deena so she wouldn't have to make the long, uphill walk to the inn by herself, but when she heard Deena discussing with Serious Stewart the origins of drama in the ancient church, she knew that she'd better start home alone.

* * *

"You're out of bounds!" Johnny said as Kathy looked at him from the other side of the kitchen table. "I haven't touched your earphones." He took a quick bite of his mashed potatoes. "Besides," he added, just slightly before he swallowed his mouthful, "I couldn't even find 'em if I wanted to in that pile of socks and scarves . . . "

"O.K., Johnny," Kathy interrupted, "no need to . . . "

" . . . and jeans and sweaters and T-shirts and underpants . . . " Johnny started his giggling.

"Johnny!" Kathy pointed her fork menacingly at her little brother as he began laughing wildly.

" . . . and shoes and . . . pantyhose!"

"Johnny!" said Lydia sternly. "Take it easy. Now"—she turned to Deena—"what was it you wanted to tell me when I was on the phone right before dinner?"

Deena looked over at Kathy and winked. "Well, Kathy and I both have something pretty special to announce," she said. "It's about the school play."

"What play?" asked Nancy.

"It's *The Sound of Music*," Deena told everyone. "Kathy's got the part of Lisl and—"

"Kathy!" Lydia smiled at her niece. "This is wonderful news! I didn't know you'd gone out for the play."

"Well . . . " Kathy shrugged.

"It's a surprise to me, too, honey," said Nancy. "This is quite a . . . change of pace for you, isn't it?"

"It's not exactly the Grateful Dead," admitted Kathy, "but it's . . . music."

"AND," Deena announced, "I've been made the assistant director!"

"Congratulations!" Lydia and Nancy said together.

"Thank you," said Deena, beaming.

"And Deena thinks the director is no toad," Kathy interjected.

Deena ignored the intention of Kathy's remark, but picked up on the subject. "Stewart Sharkey is the director," she said. "He's a senior, and last year he directed *Fiddler on the Roof* and *The Pajama Game*. When he was a sophomore, he was assistant director on *The King and I* and *Finian's Rainbow*."

"I heard he was hoping to do *The Rocky Horror Picture Show* this year," Kathy cracked.

"So," said Lydia, "when's the big performance? We want to put this on our calendars."

"March twenty-first is opening night. Just four weeks from tomorrow," said Deena. "And I know it's going to be a hit!"

* * *

After dinner, after dishes, and after a long, hot soak in the tub, Kathy snowplowed the clothes on her bed onto the floor and flopped down to read her script. Rapidly she skipped through the pages until she came to Lisl's first part. She put a little check mark next to it and flipped down to her next line. No way she was going to read this whole two-ton script.

Deena handed yellow and pink highlighters to Kathy. "Make your work soooo much easier," she said.

Kathy sighed and took the markers. The light pink, she thought, would make a nice addition to the NUCLEAR WASTE lettering on her notebook.

Deena still stood beside Kathy's bed, fidgeting. At last she said, "Why don't I listen to you read your part? We could get a head start on the first rehearsal."

"Oh, I don't think I have the energy for it tonight . . . " Kathy began. She was thinking about Roy and that awful sound of his motorcycle fading into the distance.

"Now"—Deena didn't seem to have heard Kathy—"the way I see Lisl is that she is the eldest of seven children without a mother, so she's taken on the role of mother, but at the same time she still needs and very much *wants* a mother. This is why she has been the ringleader in torturing the governesses that their father keeps hiring to take care of them." Deena asked, "Is that consistent with your image of the character?"

"I guess," said Kathy, looking at Deena weirdly. "You've really given Lisl a lot of thought, haven't you?"

"Well," Kathy thought she saw Deena's face redden. "Lisl *is* a wonderful character, so it wasn't hard to get into her head and, you know, sort of be the way she'd be, act the way she'd act, think the way she'd think."

"So that's your trick," said Kathy. "Just turn into the character."

"Oh, you know what I mean!" Deena giggled at herself. "I guess I do get carried away sometimes. Anyway, you want to go over the lines?"

"O.K." Kathy sighed. "I guess we could go through some. But not too many, O.K.? It's been a long day."

"Let's begin on page seventeen. I'll read Rolf's lines," said Deena, suddenly rather stiff, Kathy thought.

Kathy began reading and, it seemed to her, that Deena had a valuable insight to share for every line, sometimes every word. Kathy tried to grit her teeth and read on, but reading through clenched teeth didn't do much for Lisl's character.

"Remember," cautioned Deena, "she's basically an innocent girl, a good girl, who's simply overwhelmed by her family responsibilities and with the feelings that come with first love—her crush on Rolf. Now, try it again."

Kathy buried her face in her pillow. She was an innocent girl, too! A good girl, who was overwhelmed not only by her family responsibilities, but also hounded by Mrs. D. and forced to participate in some Goody Two-shoes play while her first love's feelings for her were evaporating into thin air. Yes, Kathy thought, I can identify with Lisl. But not tonight.

"No more!" she wailed. "Enough!"

Chapter 11

"Have a seat in the front two rows so I can see you for the read-through. Just stand when you read your part," Stewart suggested at the first rehearsal. Deena thought this was a brilliant idea.

In fact, so many of Stewart's ideas, as well as her own, seemed brilliant lately. It seemed to Deena that her life had actually begun when Stewart Sharkey told her that he had selected her to be the assistant director of *The Sound of Music*. None of her other responsibilities could hold a candle to this new one, not Pep Club or Student Council or French Club or even Ski Club. In fact, it hadn't been a hard decision at all to choose between attending the French Club dinner at Chez René and being at rehearsal: The play came first.

Deena went over and took the empty seat beside Ken, who was bent over his script.

"How's it going?" Deena asked cheerily.

"Hey, Deena," said Ken, looking up at her. "Oh, it's going great. I've got Rolf's lines down, no problem."

"That's great!" said Deena. "How about the song?"

Ken shook his head. "I haven't started working on that yet." He gave her a long look. "Maybe I'll need some sort of individual coaching on the song."

A smile crept to Deena's lips. "That could be arranged," she whispered as she stood up and headed for her official position, sitting on the stage next to Stewart.

Then Margaret McCabe stood and launched the rehearsal with a monologue about the hills and the sky and the air. Deena thought it was a dazzling interpretation of the character of Maria. She nodded at Margaret in a way that she hoped conveyed her high opinion.

Next came Lauren Richardson's speech about Maria not being an asset to the abbey.

"A bit more . . . how shall I put it?" Deena interjected when Lauren finished. "Holy," Deena said at last. "See if you can give it a more spiritual quality."

Kathy was glad she was not Lauren Richardson. If she were, she might have to say a few things to Ms. Deena-Director which were not all that holy or spiritual. Looking critically at her notebook, she realized she had finished her masterpiece of NUCLEAR WASTE. She cocked her head slightly as she admired her work.

"O.K.!" The voice of Stewart Sharkey rose once more. "Let's begin the scene where Rolf delivers the telegram to von Trapp's butler. Ken? You and Justin ready?"

Ken began his read-through. Deena listened intently. She imagined that Stewart would have plenty of constructive criticism for Ken. But by the time the scene finished, Stewart was deep in conversation with Ms. Pope. Well, Deena thought, it was up to her.

"You're just delivering a telegram, it's true," she reminded him. "But you have already been associating with the Nazis, and everything about you should speak of your commitment to the movement. You need to be more . . . rigid, more formal, more . . . militaristic."

Kathy fully expected Ken to get a little bit militaristic and tell Deena where to get off, but instead he nodded silently and tried the scene again, just the way Deena had asked him to. At the end he said, "Thanks for the input, Deena. That was better." Deena smiled and relaxed a little.

Kathy wanted to scream. She wanted to leap up, heave her script, and race out of the auditorium. What was she doing here, anyway, surrounded by twerps who said things like "Thanks for the input"?

"Kathy?" Serious Stew was calling her name. "I want to hear the bit where you excuse yourself from the dinner table and go out to meet Rolf. Got your place?"

Kathy flipped through her script. "Got it," she said.

Instead of throwing herself out of the chorus room, Kathy took a deep breath and threw herself into the part of Lisl. Deena's words rang in her ears. *An innocent girl, a good girl.* Kathy tried to read that way, but it just didn't work. She heard herself sounding falsely cheery, sickeningly sweet. When she and Ken came to the point where their song started, they stopped the reading. The room was still. Kathy looked up and met Deena's eyes.

Why, why, *why* does it have to be Deena up there? Kathy asked herself. Why couldn't it be anybody else but Miss Prisspot, Know-It-All, Bossy Deena?

"Well, for a first time through," Deena began cheerily, "I'd say it wasn't too bad. But, Lisl . . . How can I put this?" Deena paused. "I don't think the essence of your character has yet been grasped. Lisl *is* innocent, but she is lively and very thrilled about her first crush."

Crush! That was just what Kathy felt like doing to Deena! The "essence of her character!" Kathy didn't think she was going to be able to take Ms. Deena in her managerial capacity for a whole month. She really didn't.

"Thank you, Kathy and Ken," Stewart said. "O.K., who's in the next scene?"

Kathy sat down. She thought that if she were a cartoon character, smoke would start pouring out of the top of her head to show that she was burning up inside with anger. Who did Deena think she was, anyway? Kathy stared at her script and tried to think about something else, anything else. *A subatomic attraction, baby*, Kathy tried out the words in her head, but she couldn't even remember the next line.

As she sat there, a long dark shadow by the doorway caught her eye. She looked up and thought she saw the hem of Mrs. Dietrich's suit disappearing down the corridor. Suddenly it all came back to her—an avalanche of reasons why she was sitting in that seat and why she was going to be sitting there for the next few weeks.

Kathy listened as Jennifer Wing read through the part of Louisa, Captain von Trapp's middle daughter. At the end came the assistant director's critique. "That was fine, just fine for a read-through, Jennifer," Deena said. "Next time, think about your own childhoc and then try to get the Louisa inside you to come out and speak for you."

Jennifer nodded as though what Deena had said made perfect sense to her. "Thank you," she said.

Kathy couldn't believe it.

Chapter 12

The first week of rehearsals ended at last. Kathy thought a week had never crawled by so slowly. She'd been looking forward to the weekend the way little kids look forward to Christmas. But when Saturday morning arrived, it wasn't exactly the way she pictured it. Her mother awakened her at nine o'clock and told her to report to the kitchen A.S.A.P.

"What is this," groaned Kathy, "women's prison?"

"Just a little pitching in," her mother had said. Kathy didn't like the sound of that.

In the kitchen Kathy barely had time to gobble a small piece of coffee cake before her mother thrust a big sponge into her hand. She gave Deena a roll of paper towels.

"It's gotta be done, kids," Nancy said. "Guests are arriving at the end of the week, so we don't have that much time to get things shipshape. It's this or scrape paint off the walls of the blue bathroom."

Kathy'd had it with paint removal. She still had flecks of pink paint in her hair from scraping the walls of the pink bathroom. She took the big bucket of water her mother had just filled and glared at the oversized black oven. Deena tore off a paper towel and dampened it.

"It's already been sprayed with oven cleaner," Nancy informed her work crew. "You just have to wipe it clean."

"Just," huffed Kathy. The inside of the oven looked as big as a cave. "Some day off," she grumbled as she stuck the sponge in the sink.

"Let's just get it over with," said Deena with a sigh. "And, hey! We could go over some lines from the play while we work," she suggested.

Kathy slapped her sponge down on the kitchen counter. "No way," she said. "Even if working like Cinderella is our moms' idea of how we should spend our weekend, I'd like—just mentally—to take a break from everything having to do with school, including the p-l-a-y." She knelt and stuck her head inside the oven. "Whew! Think this stuff is carcinogenic, or what!"

"Really!" said Deena, kneeling next to Kathy. "You know, Kathy, sometimes you almost sound as if you don't like being in the play."

Kathy sponged off a section of muck from the oven ceiling and squeezed out her sponge in a bucket of water. "Sometimes I don't," she admitted.

Deena wiped away at the oven walls with her wad of damp toweling and shook her head. "But *why*?" she asked. "It's such an honor to be a part of this old Cranford tradition! Did you know that the cast pictures from every production are up in the administration building? We'll be up there, too!"

"Whoopie." Kathy reached farther into the oven. "But you," she said, "you're having a great time, aren't you?"

"I love it!" admitted Deena. "Why shouldn't I?"

"It's perfect for you," said Kathy. "You get to tell everyone what to do!"

"That's my *job*!" Deena protested. "A director has to direct!"

"That's what I said," Kathy went on, unable to stop now what she knew was leading to trouble. "It's perfect for you. But for those of us who are always being told what to do, it's not so thrilling."

"I see," said Deena from between clenched teeth. "Well, Kathy, now that I understand how you feel, I'll be glad to stop telling you what to do."

"That would be just super," said Kathy. Seeing that her sponge was saturated once again with grime, she turned to dunk it in her bucket. Unfortunately, Deena chose the same moment to try for a splotch on the back wall of the oven. *Thwack*! Kathy's sponge and Deena's face collided.

"Hey!" Kathy cried. "It was an accident! I swear, Deena!"

Deena shot up. A wide black smear nearly covered her face. She looked fiercely at Kathy, but she didn't yell. She was afraid that if she opened her mouth, she'd find out what oven cleaner tasted like. She rushed to the sink and began splashing water all over her face.

Kathy ran to the sink behind her. "Deena, I'm really sorry!" she insisted. "Can I help?"

Deena just shook her head, and even when she could talk, when she was drying her face on her paper towels, she chose not to. Instead, she walked out of the kitchen, leaving the oven to her Cranberry Cousin.

* * *

For the next week Deena popped out of bed each dawn, eager as a bluebird to face a new day. She handled dozens of challenges as assistant director. She had a clipboard, which she was never seen without, and on it she organized everything conceivable about *The Sound of Music*: props, costumes, make-up, entrance cues, and—her own invention—line coaching. And she did it all without ever saying a word to Kathy.

During this same week Kathy was about as eager to pop out of bed as a hibernating bear in midwinter. In fact, that's just what she felt she was doing, hibernating. Most mornings she had to leave for school while it was still dark in order to attend Deena's special coaching sessions, required for any actors who were not 100 percent sure of their parts. Deena had Rachel Laplant helping Kathy. Though Kathy had tried to apologize a dozen times, Deena wouldn't listen. Finally Kathy gave up. At least Deena wasn't telling her what to do anymore.

Then, after school, instead of buzzing around Cranford on the back of a bike, feeling the good, cold fresh air hitting her face, she had to trudge off to the auditorium for script practice or down the steps to the near-subterranean chorus room for singing practice. By the time rehearsal was over, it was dark outside again.

If it hadn't been for the singing practices, Kathy would have called it quits. But the singing kept her alive. It wasn't hard rock by any stretch of the imagination, but there was something about the singing that made Kathy feel good. Margaret McCabe had gotten the breathiness out of her voice and was doing a really great Maria. And Kathy's song, "I Am Sixteen," wasn't sounding all that bad, either. In fact, after the last practice, Margaret had even "honored" her by nodding in her direction!

But on this Thursday afternoon there hadn't been a singing practice and everything had seemed to go wrong. Stewart, whom she had now nicknamed Sour Stew, had spent the entire time working with the children of Captain von Trapp. It seemed so absurd. Everyone knew their lines pretty well. But Stewart relentlessly put them through their parts over and over again.

After rehearsal Kathy threw on her pea coat, wrapped her bright yellow scarf around her neck, pulled on the black suede gloves that she'd found at the bottom of a barrel in a thrift shop, and headed out the door. To her surprise, she nearly bumped into Roy.

"Hey!" she said, her face coming back to life. She gave him a hug. "I thought I might never see you again."

"I know," Roy said, slipping an arm around Kathy's middle and ushering her up the stairs. "But I had to come and tell you the great news!" He grinned at Kathy. "Got time to stop by the Hut for a slice?"

"I'll make time," said Kathy. "Wait right here. Don't move, O.K.?"

Roy nodded.

Kathy ran to the chorus room to find Deena, who was in the middle of coaching Dee Dee Goffstein on how a Reverend Mother could be both assertive and passive.

"Deena," Kathy whispered, interrupting her cousin and making her pay attention, "could you please, *please* tell my mom I'm going to be kind of late tonight? I've got to talk to someone. It's real important."

Deena gave Kathy a long look. Then she nodded.

Kathy spun around and raced out of the room. She grabbed Roy by the elbow, and the two of them ran out together. Kathy took a deep sniff of the cold, crisp air. "Ahhh!" he said. "I feel like I've just escaped from prison!"

Roy started up his bike and Kathy got on. They drove through the bustling streets of Cranford to the Pizza Hut just at the edge of town.

Walking into the toasty warm restaurant, smelling of tomato sauce and cheese, Kathy thought it was almost worth it to be working so hard on the play because it felt so good just to stop for a while. Roy led the way to what had once been their favorite booth in the corner.

"Yo, Katherine!" said Fred, Pizza Hut's finest waiter. "Long time no see."

"Hey, Fred!" said Kathy. "How 'bout a slice with pepperoni and a Sprite?"

"The same for me," said Roy, "only I'd like two slices with sausage, hold the pepperoni, and a large Coke."

Fred rolled his eyes at Roy. "Always the comedian," he muttered as he jotted down their order.

"So"—Kathy took Roy's hand across the table—"what's the big surprise?"

"The big surprise is—" Roy began.

"Ellecia and Zee," Kathy finished for him as the two friends appeared behind Roy and plopped themselves down in the booth.

"Hi," said Ellecia, giving a friendly snap with her gum. "Kath, I can't believe I'm seeing you. You for real?"

"I'm for real, all right," said Kathy. "That play is a killer, though. Next week we start rehearsals every single night, even Friday!"

"Friday nights?" Ellecia looked like she might blow her wad of gum out of her mouth on the *f-f-f* in Friday, but she saved it at the last minute.

"Are you serious?" cried Zee. "You won't even make it home in time for Rock Videos? Man, that's cruel and unusual!"

"Definitely." Kathy shrugged. "Oh, well, it'll be over in a couple more weeks." She looked mischievously at Roy. "You all *are* going to get tickets so you can see me live and on stage, aren't you?"

"For sure," said Ellecia.

"Depending on when it is," said Zee.

"Speaking of tickets," said Roy, leaning back as Fred laid their slices and drinks on the table in front of them. "You'll never guess . . . "

"You order?" Fred eyed Ellecia and Zee.

"Nothing for me," said Ellecia.

"I'm into anorexia," Zee informed the waiter.

Fred gave Zee an evil glare and walked off.

Kathy turned back to Roy. "Tickets?" she prompted him. "Tickets?"

Roy reached into his pocket. He pulled out two thin red strips of cardboard and tossed them on the tabletop.

"Tickets," Kathy spun the tickets around to face her and pulled them closer, " . . . the Wasteland Tour!" She looked up at Roy, stunned. "You got tickets? The tour? Nuclear Waste?" she managed.

Roy was grinning like crazy.

"Oh, wow!" said Ellecia, picking up a ticket.

"How'd you do it?" demanded Zee, grabbing the tickets from Ellecia.

"Don't rip the merchandise," cautioned Roy.

Zee ignored him and continued to stare at the tickets. "I heard they were sold out in Burlington the minute they went on sale last fall!"

"I have my sources," Roy said mysteriously.

"Must have cost you a bundle," Zee went on. "A megabundle."

Kathy was still speechless. This was a dream come true. Nuclear Waste coming to Burlington, Vermont! Just an hour's drive from Cranford! And Roy had tickets! "It's . . . it's unbelievable!" she murmured at last.

"Can you imagine seeing them in person?" Ellecia sighed and looked at Roy.

"Roy, if Kathy gets deathly ill, will you take me instead?" Zee whined.

"I'm feeling pretty healthy," Kathy growled. She picked up a ticket, too. "How long do I have to wait?" She examined the small print. "March twenty-first." The date had a nice sound to it. A kind of familiar sound. Maybe it was someone's birthday? "March twenty-first," she repeated. "Is that a Saturday?"

"Right," said Roy. "I've already got it all planned. I can borrow my mom's car. We'll leave here around four, get to Burlington in an hour, grab a bite, and be inside the Dunbar Theater by eight."

It was the word *theater* that did it, that reminded Kathy why March twenty-first had that certain ring to it. "Oh, no!" she gasped. "It can't be!"

"What?" Roy grabbed Kathy's hand as it fell heavily

to the table. "Kathy! What's the matter?"

Kathy put her arms on the table and pressed her head into them. "Everything!" came the muffled answer.

"But what?" cried Ellecia.

Zee was scanning the ticket Kathy had held for information. "What! What!" she shrieked. "You aren't allowed to go to Burlington! Your mom's grounded you? You already got something on the twenty-first? What!?" Zee's eyes darted from Roy's worried fact to Kathy's mop of brown hair on the table. Suddenly she cried, "I've got it! It's that play you're in, isn't it? It's that play!"

Roy, Ellecia, and Zee looked at Kathy's head. For a while nothing happened, but then they saw the hair nod a yes. Slowly Kathy raised her head. "It's that play," she echoed. "That stupid, smarmy, Goody Two-shoes excuse of a play opens on March twenty-first."

"But Kathy . . . " Roy could see tragedy written across Kathy's face. He didn't want to add to her misery, but wait a minute here! This wasn't just some medium-good metal band he'd gotten tickets for. This was Nuclear Waste! This was the top, the best, the out-and-out stars of the rock world! Besides which, he'd called in a lot of favors for these tickets.

Kathy banged her fist on the table. "*Why*?" she said. "Why does it have to be the same night?"

"So," said Ellecia, "what're you gonna do?"

"I don't know!" Kathy answered.

"You don't know?" Roy said, sounding as if he couldn't believe what he had heard. "You don't know? Yes, you do, Kathy! You're going to go to whoever's in charge of the play and get out of it, that's what." Roy raised his hands in a gesture that said "What's the big deal?"

Kathy shut her eyes and took a long breath. "It's not that easy, Roy," she said softly. "Sure, I could do it, but I'd be letting a lot of people down." The face of little Ms. Pope floated into her mind. "But I could," she repeated, as if to convince herself. "I could."

"Sure you could," Roy encouraged.

"Maybe she couldn't," suggested Zee.

"She could," said Roy firmly. "It'll blow over, no one will remember anything about this play, but how could you ever forgive yourself for giving up the chance to see Nuclear Waste?"

"Oh, come on! They'll be back one of these days," argued Zee. "They tour like totally all the time!"

Kathy held her hands up as if to push Roy's and Zee's words away. "O.K., O.K., enough," she said. "I just have to think about it, that's all. I just have to think about it."

Roy wiggled the tickets in front of Kathy's nose.

"Fifth row center," he said.

"Oooohhhhh," groaned Kathy. She stood up. "Come on, Roy. I've got to get going." She gave a wave. "See you, Ellecia, Zee."

"See you," said Ellecia, folding a fresh stick of gum and adding it to her already hefty wad.

"And, hey, Roy?" Zee chirped.

Roy turned. "Yeah?"

"Just remember," Zee told him with a meaningful look, "I don't have to think about it."

Chapter 13

Deena was sitting in the dark on the window seat watching Ken's back as he headed down the hill away from the inn. Just as she had dreamed he would, Ken had asked if he could walk her home after rehearsal. All the way they'd talked about the play, about how it was going and how privileged they felt to be a part of Cranford's outstanding dramatic tradition. It felt so good to share things with Ken. The two of them felt just the same about so many things. And then, just outside the front door, Ken had looked into her eyes and then slowly bent down to kiss her. Ken's lips were soft and sweet. Deena's heart skipped a beat when she thought of it. Their first kiss, the first of many, she hoped. After Deena had let herself into the inn, she had run right up to her room so she could see Ken walking home.

Deena was still sitting by the window, daydreaming, when Roy's bike pulled up outside the inn and Kathy got off. Deena ducked behind the curtain. She *wasn't* spying. After all, she'd already been at the window when they arrived. What was Kathy doing, she wondered, talking a mile a minute and making those wild gestures? She wished she could hear better. Maybe if she opened the window just a crack. But, no, that *would* be spying, wouldn't it? And anyway, here came Kathy walking slowly up the sidewalk. She doesn't look too happy, Deena thought. Not happy at all.

Deena turned away from the window. She paced her side of the room. Ever since Ken's kiss, she felt warm and kind of mellow. Now she felt bad about ignoring Kathy all week. Kathy had tried to apologize, and the sponge hitting her in the face like that probably was an accident. But it hadn't been the sponge that had gotten Deena so furious. It was what Kathy had said, about how great she was at telling everybody what to do. She was a take-charge type. Deena admitted that. And so was Stewart Sharkey. In fact, since she'd been working with Stewart, she'd gotten just a teensy taste of what it was like to be taken charge of, and she wasn't all that wild about it herself. Even though Stewart was very intelligent and dynamite looking, Deena was starting to feel that he was just too bossy.

Deena was still pacing when Kathy shoved open the door to their room and plodded in.

Kathy didn't look at Deena. She dropped her books to the floor and collapsed onto her bed.

"Kathy!" Deena's all-is-forgiven voice made Kathy look up.

Deena walked over and sat down on the edge of her cousin's bed. "What's wrong?"

"You name it," said Kathy, sighing.

"O.K.," said Deena, taking Kathy's invitation to name it literally. "You and Roy had a fight?"

"Partly," groaned Kathy. "Roy got concert tickets, to Wasteland, Nuclear Waste's big tour."

"Well, that's *great* news!" Then Deena grew puzzled. "Isn't it?"

"It would be," said Kathy, "if the concert weren't on the night of March twenty-first."

"Oh, no," said Deena. "Our opening night."

Kathy turned over on her back and stared at a crack in the ceiling. "*The Sound of Music*," she said thoughtfully. "What I'd really like to do is hear the sound of Nuclear Waste's music."

"That is bad luck," conceded Deena. "But look at the bright side . . . "

"The *bright* side?" Kathy sat up straight. "The bright side? *What* bright side, Deena? There isn't a bright side to this mess! It doesn't have a bright side!"

"All I meant," Deena began, "was that, well . . . " Deena looked thoughtful. "I guess you're right," she said at last. "There *doesn't* seem to be a bright side." She twisted her gold signet ring and tried to think what she could say. She wondered again about why Kathy had tried out for *The Sound of Music* in the first place. Surely she knew how demanding the rehearsal schedule would be, that there would be social opportunities she'd have to say no to. "Was Roy upset when you told him you couldn't go?" she asked at last.

"Upset would be putting it mildly," Kathy said, not daring to confess that Roy fully expected her to bail out of the play and go to the concert.

Deena racked her brain to find some words to comfort her cousin, but it wasn't easy. At last she said, "Well, you know everyone thinks you're doing a great job as Lisl. Especially with the song."

Kathy could tell Deena meant to be kind. "Thanks," she said. But, in fact, it wasn't much comfort.

* * *

"Now," said Mrs. Godfrey the following Friday morning in English, "we're going to do a read-through of *Macbeth* next week, just for fun. So, who'd like to read the title role? Matt? O.K. And Lady Macbeth? Ellecia, was your hand up? No? Well, why don't you take this role anyway? Yes, you can. You'll do fine. Just get rid of that gum. Oh, and since these parts are so big and the reading will take place over the next few days, let's have some volunteers to be understudies for Macbeth and Lady Macbeth."

Kathy had only been half-listening to Mrs. Godfrey. She'd been mostly turning her number-one problem over in her mind, as she had been for a week now. Here it was, Friday the thirteenth, the day she'd promised Roy she'd let him know what she was going to do about the concert. And she still didn't know! She didn't think she had the guts to quit the play cold just a week and a day before it opened, but she didn't have the heart to say no to Nuclear Waste—and to Roy.

That's why, the minute Mrs. Godfrey had said the word *understudies*, Kathy felt as if a lightning bolt had hit her. That was it! That was all she needed to get her out of her dilemma—an understudy! That way she wouldn't have to quit the play; she could just go on rehearsing for it. Then on opening night, she'd give her understudy the opportunity all understudies hope for: the chance to go on stage while she, Kathy, went to the concert with Roy.

All she had to do, Kathy figured, was to let Ms. Pope know right away, right after English, that she desperately needed an understudy. When she thought about it, it was sort of careless of Ms. Pope not to have arranged it already. Kathy fidgeted through the rest of English class so much that Mrs. Godfrey thought she was raising her hand and gave her the part of Hecate, the head witch.

"Kath! Wait up!" Ellecia called as class ended, and Kathy bolted for the door.

"I'll catch you later!" Kathy called back, speeding down the hall toward the steps. She had to catch Ms. Pope before next period began.

Kathy thought she might have made record time going from the second floor all the way down to the chorus room. There she found Ms. Pope, standing beside the piano, looking slightly dazed.

Kathy ran up to her but found that she was so out of breath that she couldn't utter a single word. She just stood there, panting at Ms. Pope.

"Hi, Kathy," said Ms. Pope, rather absently. "I just can't believe it. We've never had anything like this happen before. Ever."

Kathy had caught her breath enough to say, "What?"

Ms. Pope shook her head. "Oh, I forgot," she said. "None of you cast members knows yet, do you?"

"Knows what?" A glimmer of hope began to rise inside Kathy. From the looks of Ms. Pope's face, something terrible had happened, and it had to do with the play. Maybe she wouldn't need an understudy after all.

"About Margaret," said Ms. Pope mournfully. "Her mother called this morning and told me that Margaret's sprained her neck! She's going to be in bed for a week and then in a neck brace for two months!"

Kathy tried to look horrified. "That's just awful!" she said. And then she added, "She didn't have an understudy, did she?"

"No, no." Ms. Pope waved one hand in the air above the piano. "We've never bothered with understudies. I've always felt it was too much to ask for a student to learn a part well enough to play it and then not get to. No, she didn't have an understudy."

"Well," said Kathy, still trying to hide her feelings of joy, "I guess we'll have to call off the play."

Ms. Pope's hand flew to her heart. "Don't even say such a thing! Of course we'll have the play. The show must go on!"

"But who . . . " Kathy began.

"Somehow," said Ms. Pope dramatically, "we will find another Maria."

"You know," said Kathy, quickly remembering why she had come to talk to Ms. Pope in the first place, "it might not be a bad idea to have understudies for this performance. I know it would make me feel better if I had one for Lisl."

Ms. Pope gave a little shrug and waved her hand around again. "I think we have enough to worry about now with Margaret on the disabled list, don't you?"

"I guess you're right," said Kathy, now feeling as glum

as she had tried to look when she had heard the news about Margaret's neck. "Well, I have to go. See you at rehearsal."

"Bye, Kathy," said Ms. Pope, and then, looking up, she added, "Oh, hello, Arlene."

Kathy saw that Mrs. Dietrich had stepped into the chorus room. "Hello, Mrs. Dietrich," said Kathy as she approached the door.

"Good afternoon," Mrs. D. said with a nod to each of them. "Well, how's it going with the play?"

"Just great," said Kathy, making herself slim as she wedged her body around Ms. Dietrich's to get out the door. "Really, just great!"

***

Kathy sat limply at her desk as the Friday bell sounded to end another week at Cranford High. She knew what would happen if she got up. She would walk out of the classroom, down the hallway, and to her locker, where Roy would be waiting to hear her answer: that she'd gotten out of doing the play and was willing, ready, and able to go to the concert with him. How can I tell him that I just can't do that? she wondered. How can I make him understand?

"Kathy?" Mr. Millander's bulky form stood beside Kathy's desk. "Planning to camp out here this weekend?"

"No," Kathy said as she pulled herself up reluctantly and started going through the motions that destiny had in store for her. "I just ran out of energy, I guess."

"You have been working hard lately," Mr. Millander

commented as Kathy strode toward the door. "You get my vote for most improved student in American history."

Kathy stopped in her tracks and turned. "Really?" she said.

Mr. Millander nodded. "Really."

For some reason this made Kathy feel good. She smiled at her teacher. "Well, thanks for letting me know, Mr. Millander."

The hallway was nearly empty as Kathy walked slowly to her locker. Just as she had predicted, Roy was leaning against the locker next to hers.

Before she had even reached him, Kathy called out, "I didn't do it, Roy. I couldn't do it! I am a total chicken, and I don't deserve to see Nuclear Waste because I can't make myself"—she lowered her voice—"get out of the play!"

Roy looked as if Kathy had just dealt him a solid right to the jaw followed by a left hook to the abdomen.

Kathy leaned her head against her locker and banged it against the cold metal several times. It clanged loudly, echoing in her ears. By the time she'd had enough she looked up and caught sight of Roy's back, disappearing around the corner.

Chapter 14

"I have a sad announcement to make," said Ms. Pope that afternoon as the cast assembled in the first two rows of the auditorium for Friday afternoon rehearsal. "Margaret McCabe has injured herself and will not be able to continue as Maria."

"No!" Deena's voice lead the others as she gasped this single syllable of shock. Then a general tumult of disbelief broke out.

"It can't be!"

"What'll we do?"

"What happened to her, Ms. Pope?"

"I believe . . . that is . . . her mother informed me," said Ms. Pope, "that Margaret has sprained her neck."

"Her neck?"

"Can't she play it with a neck brace?"

"Ms. Pope! How'd it happen?"

"How did she do it?"

"Well," Ms. Pope answered, "I'm really not all that clear on the details. Her mother said something about

Margaret seeing some people she knew in some automobiles on Conway Road."

"Was she in a car accident?"

"No, no," said Ms. Pope in an agitated manner. "Not exactly. I believe her mother said that Margaret was walking on the side of the road, and she was waving to someone she knew when she saw someone *else* she knew coming from the other direction and when she quickly turned to wave to them, her neck . . . just . . . stuck."

The cast was quiet for a long moment, trying to picture exactly how it was that Margaret had gotten her neck stuck.

Then Dee Dee Goffstein's voice piped up. "But Ms. Pope! How can we do the play without Maria?"

"We won't do the play without Maria," Ms. Pope said firmly. "We'll simply have to find another Maria."

More surprised comments resulted from Ms. Pope's answer.

"But who?"

"No one can do it like Margaret."

"There's barely a week left for someone to learn the whole part!"

And then suddenly, above the chatter, a voice arose.

"I know who could take the part, Stewart!" It was Lauren Richardson. "Deena Scott!"

Deena flashed Lauren a smile. "Thanks, Lauren, but I don't know . . . " she stammered. "It's . . . "

"You can do it, Deena!" Lauren was looking at her and nodding. Then she turned to Stewart. "Have you ever heard her read the scene with Captain von Trapp? It's fantastic!"

"Really!" added Dee Dee Goffstein. "When she

helped me with my lines, I heard her read, too, and I think she'd make a great Maria!"

"She'd be wonderful!"

"Deena!"

"She'd be just right!"

"Perfect!"

Deena's head was spinning. She shook her head to clear it and then looked over at Stewart. He was staring at her and looked as if he were thinking—very hard.

"I'll make any casting decisions here," Stewart said at last. "Deena, I'd like to hear what you can do. Why don't you read through the scene where the Captain and Maria discuss the children having signals. Gerard? I'd like you to do your lines with Deena."

Taking a breath to calm herself and setting down her clipboard, Deena walked up the steps to the stage. She stood next to Gerard. "Ready when you are," she said.

"Um," Gerard whispered, "don't you want a script?"

Deena shook her head. "Not necessary," she said, and then she began speaking Maria's opening lines.

At first Kathy could feel tension from the rest of the cast with Deena up in front of them on the stage doing her own interpretation of Maria. She was nothing like the breathy, blond Maria as played by Margaret McCabe. But by the time Deena finished her last line, there was a spontaneous burst of applause from the first two rows, led by a loud "Bravo!" from Stewart Sharkey.

"Deena!" called Ms. Pope from the front-row seat into which she had collapsed when she heard Deena doing such a marvelous Maria.

"You've got it!" announced Stewart. "The part is yours!"

Even Kathy had to agree Deena had swept her away as Maria. In some respects, she was much better than Margaret McCabe. It was hard to believe that smiling, nodding Margaret would ever have been a nun in the first place. But Deena played Maria as a fierce and committed person, who could easily have been a sort of renegade nun. Yet something kept tugging at the back of Kathy's mind about this role for Deena. What was it? She couldn't pinpoint it and so chalked it up to her own problem of wanting to go hear Nuclear Waste versus having to stay and be a part of a nuclear family, as represented by the von Trapps.

Then, as Kathy rose from her chair to go to singing practice, the thing that had been bothering her came into focus. Deena, the able assistant director, the person who had saved the day, the new Maria . . . couldn't sing a note!

* * *

"It's true!" Deena was beaming as she looked at the circle of faces around the big oak table in the inn kitchen. "Of course I wish Margaret hadn't injured her neck, but she did, and now I'm playing the lead!"

"That's really something, honey," said Lydia, spooning some sliced beets into Johnny's plate.

"I wish Daddy could be here to see it," Deena added. "You know how much he loves music."

Kathy winced. If Deena's father loved music, she thought, better he should be spared the sound of his daughter singing in public.

"Johnny, you can't hide your beets under that bread, so forget it," said Lydia.

"Go ahead and try a beet," encouraged Nancy gently.

"Low score!" complained Johnny. "These beets are full of *blood*!"

Deena let her fork fall heavily on her plate. "Do we *have* to listen to this?"

"Johnny," said Kathy, trying to think what she could say to change the subject away from bloody beets and from the play, "have you found my headphones yet?"

"Double dribble, Kath!" Johnny said. "You ask me that every night!" He shoved a sliced beet under a nest of string beans. "I keep telling you, I gave 'em back."

"O.K., O.K.," said Kathy. "I just thought maybe you'd seen them around." She gave him a wink and pointed at her beets with her fork, making a face.

Johnny understood. "Two points!" he whispered.

"We start dress rehearsals next week," Deena was telling everyone in an excited voice. "I just love the costumes Maria gets to wear." She sighed.

"You love her clothes?" Kathy couldn't help herself. "She spends the first act in a black nun's habit and then changes into a dress that she says she couldn't give to the poor because the poor didn't want it!"

Deena shrugged sheepishly. "I guess I'm just in love with anything to do with Maria," she said. "Want to practice my lines with me after dinner, Kathy?"

"I guess," said Kathy.

"You girls go ahead," said Nancy, standing up to clear the table. She whisked Johnny's beet-strewn plate away before there could be any more discussion about it. "Lydia and I can take a turn doing the dishes while we go over the menus for next week. We've got the inn booked solid!"

"That's great, Aunt Nancy," said Deena. "And thanks for your offer on the dishes. Ready, Kathy?"

"Yeah," said Kathy. "Thanks, Mom."

Upstairs the cousins got out their scripts. Kathy gave the cues, Deena recited Maria's lines that followed them. During the first act, she didn't miss one word. The second act was almost as good. Kathy only needed to coach her on the three longest speeches. At last they finished.

"Deena," Kathy ventured carefully, "what about the songs?"

"I know the songs," said Deena, full of confidence. "Every word."

"Every word," repeated Kathy. Silently she wondered, What about every note?

Chapter 15

Even though Kathy felt like a twit in her frilly white blouse and short dirndl skirt, she thought getting ready for the first dress rehearsal was exciting. There was Lauren Richardson, transformed into Sister Bernice, and Jennifer Wing, looking cute and petite in her dirndl outfit as Louisa. Even Gerard looked worldly and sophisticated in his naval uniform as Captain von Trapp.

As the cast assembled on this Wednesday, just three days before opening night, the stage crew was monkeying around with the lighting, shining spots here and there and changing the atmosphere from a sunny day to a threatening thundershower. The school orchestra, which had been practicing the songs for three weeks, was in place now, tuning up their instruments. The scene painters were securing a backdrop showing the Alps, all misty and purple in the distance, and setting little cardboard bushes and flowers in the foreground. Kathy marveled that, after all the fumbling with lines and songs, it looked as if the play was finally coming together.

"Places for the opening scene!" called Stewart. "Deena, you're stage left. Lauren, you and Dee Dee need to be ready to come on stage right after Maria's first song."

Kathy, who didn't come on until the third scene, watched as Deena took her place alone on the stage. The lighting switched from a ghastly green to a flattering pink. The orchestra was still.

"Close the curtain," commanded Stewart. "Let's do it all the way the right way. Remember, we've just got two more rehearsals after this one to get it down."

The curtains closed. After a few seconds of silence the orchestra began playing the overture. Chills ran down Kathy's spine. It seemed so real, so close. Before long every seat in the auditorium would be filled, and they would be doing this in front of a real, live audience—an audience vastly different from the one Roy and, she supposed, Ellecia or Zee would be part of on that night. Kathy shook her head to clear it of thoughts of the Nuclear Waste concert.

Just then the overture ended, and the curtains opened, revealing Deena, plucking imaginary flowers and twirling to take in the glory of the vista surrounding her. She said a few lines about the beauty of the earth and then, with the orchestra soft at first, and then getting louder and louder, Deena-Maria burst into song.

Deena had been right when she said she knew every word. She did. But the tune still wavered, just out of her reach. Especially the high notes. Kathy looked down at the wooden floor backstage. Maybe it's just me, she thought. Maybe my dad was right when he said I had a fine-tuned ear. Maybe no one else can hear how off she is.

Kathy looked up as Deena was concluding her song. Sister Lauren and Reverend Mother Dee Dee went on stage. Then Kathy caught sight of Ms. Pope standing beside Stewart. She looked panicky, and Stewart was talking seriously to her. Something was wrong. Stewart gave Ms. Pope a quick nod, and then walked out on stage holding up his hands. The orchestra stopped playing. "We need a few minutes," he announced. "Take a ten-minute break. Then we'll take it from the top at"— Stewart consulted his watch—"four-thirty."

Kathy was going to find a seat when she saw Stewart walk over to Deena and talk to her on stage. She stopped in her tracks and watched. Now Ms. Pope joined them. Kathy couldn't hear what they were saying to each other, but she was pretty sure she knew what it was. They were trying to figure out what to do about Deena's singing!

Ten minutes later the cast reassembled behind stage. Ms. Pope was still working with Deena on the stage. Now Kathy could hear every word. And so could every other actor in the play.

"Make your voice reach up, Deena," Ms. Pope said. Then she demonstrated with a little trill of high do-re-mi's.

Deena trilled after her, but her notes couldn't seem to climb up to where Ms. Pope's were. Over and over again Ms. Pope and Deena sang. And over and over again Deena's notes fell short—and flat. But Deena, to her credit, thought Kathy, seemed to be trying her hardest, not bristling under the instruction. In fact, Kathy found herself smiling slightly at the fact that now Deena was getting some of the criticism that she had dished out so generously!

At last Ms. Pope sighed and gave Deena a little pat on the back. "I can tell you're trying hard, Deena." She turned to Stewart. "Let's go ahead with the rehearsal, and Deena can just talk through songs. I'll work with her tonight after rehearsal and tomorrow." Stewart nodded. "O.K.," he called to the cast. "Places!"

From that point on the rehearsal went off without a hitch. Deena talked her songs, with great expression, and everyone else sang theirs. Kathy felt she had done pretty well on her song with Kenny, and evidently everyone else thought so, too, because the cast burst into applause after they finished it. It did, Kathy had to admit, feel great to be performing.

After rehearsal Kathy shed her costume quickly and sat down on an old couch backstage to wait and walk part of the way home with Dee Dee, since Deena would be staying late to practice her songs with Ms. Pope. She thought about reading some of her massive American history assignment while she waited for Dee Dee, but she didn't have the energy. She just laid her head back on the old couch and rested. As she sat there a grim-faced Ms. Pope and a dejected-looking Stewart Sharkey approached her.

Ms. Pope sat down beside Kathy on the couch.

"Kathy, I'd like you to come into my office for a moment," said Stewart. "Ms. Pope and I would like to talk to you."

"Sure," said Kathy, getting up off the couch and following them to a narrower door under the stage steps.

What did I do now? Kathy wondered. They look as if they're about to kick me out of the cast!

Inside the tiny office Stewart shut the door and nodded to Ms. Pope.

"Kathy," she began. "We have a problem."

Kathy's eyes opened wide.

"We need you to do something for us," said Stewart. "Something very difficult, but something that is vital to the continuance of the Cranford tradition of excellence in drama. The show must go on!"

Boy, thought Kathy. He sure can be dramatic! "Sure," she said out loud.

"How fast do you think you could learn the part of Maria?" asked Ms. Pope.

"By Saturday night?" Stewart asked. "Opening night?"

"Maria?" Kathy didn't quite understand. "But Deena's Maria."

Ms. Pope looked ill. "Deena is a wonderful Maria in the speaking parts," she began. "But she is not able to do the songs."

"But you're going to work with her!" Kathy exclaimed. "You're going to help her!"

"Frankly, I don't think any amount of help will do any good," said Ms. Pope. "Deena just doesn't have a voice that can handle this role. If only I hadn't been so overwhelmed by her speaking ability when she . . . " Ms. Pope evidently could not go on.

"But you *do* have a voice that can handle the role," Stewart said. "That's why we'd like you and Deena to switch roles."

Kathy closed her eyes. "Nooo," she moaned. "No, no, no!"

"As Lisl," Stewart continued, as though he were deaf to her protests, "Deena would only have one song, and it's a duet. I think she could get through that one. And she already knows the part. But you'll need to learn Maria by Saturday. Do you think you can do it?"

"It's not that," said Kathy. "It's, well, Deena would think . . . She's worked so hard . . . I just can't *do* that to her!"

Ms. Pope and Stewart gave each other a look of doom. Then Stewart turned to Kathy again.

"You've *got* to, Kathy!" he told her. "It's the only way the play can go on!"

"I can't!" Kathy repeated. "Why, I could never learn all she has to say! I'd be up there flubbing lines! It would *be* horrible, much worse than a slightly off-key Maria!"

"You've been hearing her lines for almost four weeks," said Stewart. "You'll be surprised, I think, by how much you've learned just from listening."

"Wait a minute!" said Kathy. "There's got to be another way. Couldn't Margaret McCabe be backstage and do the singing for Deena?"

Ms. Pope shook her head. "No, it's got to be sung by the actress herself. That's the essence of live theater—and why we have such a fine reputation here at Cranford."

"But this is an emergency!" protested Kathy.

"It wouldn't work anyway," said Stewart. "It would sound phony."

"Well, there's got to be another way," said Kathy. "Listen, maybe I could work with Deena, tonight, at home. Maybe I could show her how to do it so she won't sound so . . . flat."

For a moment neither Stewart or Ms. Pope spoke.

"All right," said Ms. Pope at last. "We'll let you try under one condition."

"Anything," promised Kathy recklessly. "Anything!"

"If it doesn't work, you take over the role."

"But—" began Kathy.

"Better start learning the lines," said Stewart. "Because unless you come through with a near miracle, you're going to find yourself in the starring role."

Kathy drew herself up to full height. "You'll see," she said determinedly. "I'm sure she'll be just great."

"O.K.," said Ms. Pope with a sigh. "I'll go ahead and work with her for a little while now. And you work with her tonight. But if she's still off-key tomorrow, you'll have to step in."

"O.K.," Kathy agreed. She nodded to Stewart and Ms. Pope and walked out of the little office, her head a whirl of battling ideas.

Chapter 16

"What's the matter, Kathy?" asked Nancy that night at dinner. "You've hardly touched your pot roast. I thought this was your favorite."

"It's great, Mom," Kathy said. "I'm just . . . nervous about the play, I guess."

Deena's plate was still full, too. "You think *you're* nervous," she said with an odd little laugh. "Ms. Pope told me so many things about my singing that I can't even remember them all." She looked at Kathy. "She also said you'd agreed to work with me tonight on the songs." Deena reddened as she said this.

"I will," said Kathy. She tried to give a confident smile. "I'm sure you'll be great."

"At the risk of getting dishpan hands," said Nancy, "I'll do the dishes so you can have more time to practice."

"Thanks, Aunt Nancy," said Deena giving her aunt a hug. "Well," she added briskly, "let's go to it!"

Kathy followed Deena up to their room. For some reason she thought of a book her father had read to her when she was very young about a train making it up a mountain because he kept saying he thought he could do it. I think I can help Deena sing, Kathy chanted inside her head. I think I can, I think I can.

Upstairs, Kathy dumped her books on the mountainous pile on her bed. She straddled her desk chair and turned to Deena. "O.K., you want to start with some warm-up exercises?"

"If that's the best way," said Deena, standing in front of Kathy like a willing pupil.

"I used to do these scales when I was singing with my band. They helped me reach those way-up-there notes. See, you alternate between high and low. Like this." Kathy began singing. "Do ti ti ti, re la la la, mi sol sol sol, fa!" Then Kathy said, "You try it."

"Do ti ti ti!"

Kathy noticed that Deena extended her neck like a howling dog to reach her ti's. "Wait," said Kathy. "Don't put your head up. Just keep looking at me."

"Do ti ti ti!"

"Your head's fine," said Kathy, "but even though you don't raise your head, you have to raise your voice. You just sang four do's."

"Do ti ti ti!" Deena sang, keeping her head level and squeaking up on the ti's.

"Well," said Kathy. "Let's go on to the next part. Re la la la."

"Re la la la. Oh, blah blah blah!" Deena sat down in a huff on a tiny space on Kathy's bed that was available. She crossed her arms on her chest. "I don't know why we should go on fooling ourselves about this singing. I'm just no good at it, no good at all!"

"We can work on it," said Kathy, desperation creeping into her voice. "It just takes practice!"

"You and I both know it's not going to work, Kathy," said Deena. Absently she picked up a bright blue T-shirt that was strewn across Kathy's bed and began folding it. "You know, when Margaret sprained her neck and, well, when Jennifer and Dee Dee thought I could step in, I felt so . . . oh, I don't know, flattered, I guess. I really thought I could do it, that I was capable of it."

"And you are!" said Kathy, watching with interest as tidy little piles began appearing on her bed. T-shirts here, slips next to them, socks and panties in what was evidently a laundry pile. Even that was neat.

"Sure," said Deena. "I can do the lines perfectly. I'll admit that. But the songs . . . I didn't realize how just because I wanted to do it, it didn't mean that I *could*. That's never happened to me before," she admitted. "Never. I've always believed that if I wanted to do something badly enough and worked hard at it, I could do it." She shook her head sadly. "But singing is different," she said. "It takes more than just wanting to. It takes talent . . . "

"Oh, Deena!" Kathy broke in. "Maybe the great singers are born with the voices, but lots of people can learn to be pretty decent singers. It just takes a little time . . . "

"And I have two days," Deena said as she pulled on a thin cord that stuck out from under a pair of pantyhose. Attached to the pantyhose Kathy saw a familiar sight.

"My headphones!" Kathy exclaimed. "You found them!"

Lovingly, Kathy untangled them from the stockings. Forgetting her troubles for a moment, she leaped up and plugged in the wire to her cassette player and switched on

Nuclear Waste. She bobbed her head to the music, and as the lyrics started, she sang along.

" 'Tell it to your shrink,
Say you think I stink,
Take another drink,
But don't mess with me . . . bop bop bop . . . when I'm in pink.' "

Suddenly Kathy whirled around and snatched off her headphones. "This is it!" she cried, lunging at Deena and attempting to put the phones around her cousin's head.

"What are you doing?" cried the startled Deena. "Please! What is this? You know I don't listen to this music!"

"Just sing along!" Kathy shouted so that Deena could hear her over Nuclear Waste.

Deena sat there listening to the words, her nose wrinkled in distaste. Then, after a bit, her head started nodding up and down, almost in time with the music.

" 'Buy yourself a mink," she began hesitatingly,
"Drink a glass of ink,
Tell me what you think,
But don't mess with me . . . bop bop bop bop . . . when I'm in pink.' "

"Yippee!" shouted Kathy. "It works!" Once more she lunged at Deena, this time to disengage her from the headphones. "It worked!" she said. "You sounded terrific!"

"But . . . " Deena looked at Kathy as if she had lost what little mind she thought she had. "What worked?"

"The headphones!" Kathy sat next to Deena on the bed.

Now there was plenty of room for her. "You can use the headphones in the play! This Walkman'll fit down the back of your dress. No one'll ever see it! We'll get a cassette of Julie Andrews singing Maria's songs in *The Sound of Music*, and when it comes time for your songs, you can flip it on and sing along! Don't you see? That way you'll stay on key and sound great! And it'll still be you singing!"

"But do you really think it'll work?" Deena asked.

"You were right on key with this tape," Kathy said. "Let's try it with another one." Kathy rummaged through the cassettes in the box under her bed. At last she pulled one up. "Here's *Pinheads*, "she said. "Let's try it."

For the rest of the evening, Kathy checked out Deena's tunefulness as she sang "Metal Goons," "Vaccination," and "Alien Forces." When she had finished, Kathy declared a total success. Deena said she had a headache.

"During lunch tomorrow, get a pass," said Kathy. "Say it's Student Council business or something. Then go to Sound Systems and get the tape. We'll have to do a little fast forwarding at rehearsal, but tomorrow night I can dupe just your songs! We can hide the headphones and the wire under your hair, no problem!" Kathy grinned and before she knew it, she was giving her cousin a big hug. Deena hugged her back.

Satisfied with her plans, Kathy plugged the earphones into her own ears and began reading her American history to the beat of Nuclear Waste's "Hot Tonight."

Deena sat down at her desk and tried to concentrate on her homework with the lyrics from "Metal Goons" running through her head.

Chapter 17

After school the next day Kathy went to put her books away. Her heart leaped when she thought she saw a familiar shape lounging next to her locker. It had spiky hair. Was it Roy? She tried not to walk fast. She didn't want to look overanxious or anything. At last she was standing next to him.

"Hey," she said, smiling.

Roy wasn't smiling. "Been missing you, Manelli," he said.

"I've been missing you, too," Kathy said. "Lots."

"You know"—Roy furrowed his brow in thought—"I'm not angry with you about being in the play or anything. It's just that I know how much you'd have loved the concert . . ."

"Please, Roy!" Kathy felt tears welling up in her eyes. "Don't talk about that. Or the play. They'll both be over next week. Can't we talk about something that's after next week?"

Roy walked next to Kathy down the hallway. He

didn't ask where she was going, but outside the auditorium he gave her arm a squeeze and, without looking at her, headed for the parking lot.

Kathy entered the auditorium. By this time, much of the cast was already in costume and milling around on the stage. Kathy saw Deena and smiled to herself. This Walkman plan of hers was ingenious! She couldn't wait to see the look on Ms. Pope's face! And maybe ol' Sour Puss Stew would even give out with a smile!

As she rushed by the stage to the dressing room, Kathy heard Stewart calling, "Places, everyone!" She ran faster and in a minute was backstage in her little dirndl, her heart beating in happy anticipation of Deena's success.

The curtain opened and revealed Deena whirling happily among the cardboard shrubbery and flowers. As the orchestra began playing Deena burst into song. She was right on key, and singing out so she'd be heard in the last row of the Cranford Memorial Theater balcony. Kathy smiled, then searched backstage to find Ms. Pope and Stewart. She found Ms. Pope, who was wearing an expression of dazed amazement. Someone tapped Kathy's shoulder and when she turned, she saw Stewart.

"I congratulate you," he whispered, serious as ever.

"Thanks," Kathy whispered back. "Doesn't she sound great?"

"Terrific," Stewart said. "I have to admit, I didn't think you could do it." He listened for a moment. "I wonder why she's just a little behind the orchestra like that. Listen. She's dragging just slightly."

Kathy heard it, too. Deena was dragging. "Well," Kathy said with nervous overcheerfulness, "that's easy enough to fix."

Kathy turned back to see Deena finish her song and walk off stage as the nuns entered. She ran around to the other side of the stage to meet her.

"You were great!" Kathy whispered. "But I think you've got to turn down the volume a bit so you can still hear the orchestra and stay with them." Kathy thought for a moment. "And I'll tell Rachel to slow down the orchestra's tempo a bit, too."

Deena nodded, then she and Kathy snuck into Stewart's tiny office and fast forwarded the tape to Deena's next song.

Just before Deena went on stage to sing again, Ms. Pope came up to Kathy with her arm around Deena's shoulders. She was all smiles. "This rehearsal's going so well," she said, "that I'm almost nervous about it. You know the old saying about a poor dress rehearsal and a great opening night—and vice versa."

Kathy nodded. "Well," she said jokingly, "you never know what can happen."

"Places for Act one, Scene six!" called Stewart.

From the wings, Kathy watched Deena-Maria get revved up for her meeting with Captain von Trapp and his seven children. She loved this part because a bus that the scenic designers had made came on the stage and Deena climbed up on it and sang while the scenery behind her changed from the abbey to Captain von Trapp's villa.

As Kathy watched, she realized that something was wrong, but it took her a minute to figure out what. This time, Deena wasn't dragging just a little behind the orchestra, she was dragging a *lot*! In fact, she was singing completely different notes from those the orchestra was playing. She sounded almost as if she were singing in slow motion!

Kathy clapped her hand to her forehead. "The batteries!" she moaned to herself. "They're running down! Why didn't I think to check them?"

Kathy heard giggles coming from behind her.

"What's she *doing*?" whispered Kristen Bopp. "She sounds so funny!"

Panic setting in, Kathy decided that she had to get Deena's attention. From stage left, she waved at Deena, trying desperately to catch her eye. But Deena, standing on the bus, just kept going on about all the things that she had confidence in, singing slower and slower and slower.

"What in the world . . ." Ms. Pope said under her breath.

Without thinking about what she was going to do, Kathy walked out on stage and bumped into Deena.

"Ooops!" she said aloud. "I thought I heard my cue." And as she bumped into Deena she gave the wire under her headphones a little jerk. "It's broken!" she whispered. "Just sing yourself."

Deena looked startled at first. But Kathy was off stage too quickly for Deena to ask her a question. As the orchestra found its place, Deena had time to look backstage. She saw Kristen and Dee Dee laughing like crazy. She saw Gerard in hysterics. She saw Ken with his hand over his mouth, trying to smother a laugh. It didn't take a genius to know who they were laughing at.

Deena felt her face flush in embarrassment. Well, she was not going to humiliate herself further by crying in front of everyone. So just as the orchestra began playing her introduction again, Deena ran off stage.

Chapter 18

"Wait!" Kathy dashed after Deena, following her cousin down two flights of stairs until she reached the big metal door of the prop room.

"Deena!" she cried. "Please! Let me in!" Kathy pounded on the door with her fist, and to her surprise the heavy door swung open slowly. She took a few tentative steps into the nearly dark room. "Deena!"

There was no answer. Kathy could barely see Deena curled up in an old, overstuffed chair that was probably used in every play where the script called for a "cozy, old-fashioned living room." Deena was facing away from Kathy, her face buried in her hands. Kathy looked around for a light switch, but saw only an ancient lamp, from the same era as the chair. She flipped the switch and was surprised to find that it worked. In the dim light Kathy closed the door and walked toward Deena.

Just as Kathy reached out to put a hand on her cousin's shoulder, Deena cried, "Leave me alone! Haven't you done enough already!"

"Deena!" cried Kathy. "I didn't know those batteries were going to run low. What do you think, that I set this up on purpose? I was trying to help you, remember?"

"All I remember," said Deena, wiping her eyes, "is that I have worked so hard on this play! And now the entire cast is laughing!" Deena flattened her hand against her chest. "At *me*! I've made a fool of myself in front of everyone—not to mention messing up the entire production by trying to play a role that I can't do!"

"But—" began Kathy.

"And *you!*" Deena burst in. "You don't even care about this play! I can tell! Sure, you go to rehearsals and go through the motions of being in it, but you don't care. Not really. But what happens? You get a great part, no problems. It's all just so easy for you, isn't it?"

"Easy!" gasped Kathy. "You think things are easy for me? You think giving up going to the concert with Roy so I could be in this stupid play was *easy*?"

Deena looked stunned at Kathy's anger.

"I just meant that things always come easy for you," Deena said in a voice that was now more controlled. "I seem to have to work twice as hard as anybody else to get the same things. You want to be in a play? You get a part. You want a boyfriend? You get one the first week we're here. You want a new outfit? You go to that bed of yours and somehow pull together something that the rest of the school is copying for the next six weeks!"

Now it was Kathy's turn to look stunned.

"I just can't believe you think that," Kathy said, sitting down on the ottoman at the foot of the overstuffed chair. "I feel like nothing's been easy for me since I moved here! Nothing! And you want to know why I really tried out for the play?" Kathy charged on. "I'll tell you. You remember that day I got called out of Godfrey's English class and had to go to Mrs. Dietrich's office?"

Deena nodded.

"Well," Kathy continued, "she had my report card in front of her, and every one of my teachers had written a bad comment about my attitude. Every single one!"

"Even Ms. Godfrey?" asked Deena. "I thought she liked you."

Kathy shrugged.

"So what happened?" asked Deena.

"So Mrs. D. made me this deal: She'd keep mum and not send the comments home for Mom to see, but I had to start trying in class in return. *Plus* I had to do something for Cranford High—the way *you* do—to show I had some school spirit."

"And this is it?" asked Deena. "This play is your attempt at school spirit?"

"That's right." Kathy sighed. "Ms. Pope gave me the idea and . . . I thought I might as well try something that had to do with music. I wanted to spare Mom the comments 'cause I thought they'd make her feel like she'd done the wrong thing in moving here."

"I don't blame you," said Deena.

Kathy sighed. "You know, I always thought you were the one who had it easy. All your activities, everyone knows you. You've got lots of friends, and Pat's a really good friend . . . "

"It's amazing," said Deena, "that you see it this way."

A knock on the door interrupted the cousins.

"Who is it?" called Deena.

"Stewart!" came a voice from the hallway. "I called a

break but I'm starting rehearsals up again at five o'clock. That's five more minutes. Be on stage!"

"We will!" called Deena sharply. Then, turning to Kathy, she added, "He's so . . . pompous!"

Kathy had to laugh. "I didn't think you'd noticed. He thinks we're all fortunate to be able to breathe the same air he's breathing!"

Deena shook her head. "So what are we going to do about the play?"

"I don't think anyone saw the Walkman wires," said Kathy, "but I guess it's too risky to try it in the play."

"If they didn't see the wires they must have thought something pretty weird was going on!" exclaimed Deena. She looked at Kathy almost shyly and giggled.

Kathy laughed, too. "It was pretty weird," she admitted. "But everyone's so frantic about the play, they'll all forget about it. Don't worry."

Abruptly, Deena got up from her chair and began pacing back and forth in the little room. Kathy recognized her cousin's brainstorming method by now. "As far as I can see," Deena muttered more to herself than to Kathy, "there's only one thing we can do about this play."

* * *

When Deena and Kathy walked back onto the stage, most of the cast members were milling around aimlessly. Sisters Kristen, Lauren, and Dee Dee were sitting on the steps taking turns with a nail file. Bud Wilmont and Ken Buckly were trading the straps on their lederhosen, each hoping for a better fit. Ms. Pope was half-sitting, half-lying in a chair off to the side of the stage, and Stewart was fanning her with one of the smaller clumps of cardboard flowers.

"I have an announcement!" Deena said loudly, almost before anyone had a chance to notice that she had returned without her costume. "We must make some cast changes before we go ahead with rehearsal. They're not too drastic, and I'm sure that we can all learn what we need to in two days. First of all, I am stepping down from the part of Maria." Deena paused before she went on. "Second, Kathy has agreed to take over the part, and I will coach her on the dialogue."

Kathy felt her face turning red as kids turned to look at her. She wondered if she should have agreed to Deena's plan. Then she wondered what choice she'd had.

"Third," Deena continued, "Lauren will play Lisl—we can get along with one less nun." Deena looked at Lauren. "Is that O.K. with you?" she asked.

"Yes!" said Lauren enthusiastically, whipping the habit off her head.

Deena turned to Stewart and the still-limp Ms. Pope. "Of course, these changes are subject to your approval, but they seemed the most logical to me."

Ms. Pope nodded her consent. Even Stewart, for the moment, was speechless.

"And I," concluded Deena, "will go back to my previous position of assistant director."

Stewart stopped fanning Ms. Pope. "Places everybody!" he called. "Act one, Scene one!"

Chapter 19

A slash of early spring sunlight crossed Kathy's face on Saturday morning, March twenty-first, but she slept soundly on. She was still sleeping like a log at ten when Nancy came into the room.

"Shhhh!" cautioned Deena from her desk where she had been going over last-minute dialogue changes and stage directions and checking a huge stack of programs to see that the cast changes had been made. "She was up until after three this morning working on her lines. I think we should let her get all the sleep she needs today."

"Were you up with her, Deena?" Nancy asked.

Deena nodded. "But it isn't the same for me. I don't have to be on stage tonight in the starring role."

For a minute Nancy thought Deena looked regretful over this fact, but the next minute Deena was going over the schedule for the day so thoroughly with Nancy that she thought she must have been imagining it.

"When she gets up," Deena was saying, "she should eat a good breakfast, something really nutritious that will fortify her all day, because she probably won't feel much like eating tonight. Then I'll work with her again on the lines from the third act, which are her weakest, and then she'll probably just about have time for a soak in the tub, and we'll have to get to school. We're supposed to be there by six."

"Sounds like a full day," Nancy commented. "Anything I can do to help?"

"Would you mind driving us to school at six?" Deena asked. "These programs are kind of heavy."

"No problem," said Nancy. She gave Deena a quick hug. "I'll be in the kitchen working on tonight's menu, and I'll try to think of something we can feed our leading lady for breakfast."

At noon Deena decided that nine hours of sleep was sufficient for her cousin.

"Kathy!" Deena said softly into her cousin's ear. "Kathy! You've got to get up! It's twelve o'clock."

"Uuummmmm," Kathy grunted into her pillow.

"Come on!" encouraged Deena. "You can't sleep all day!"

"Why not?" came the muffled reply.

"We've got some more work to do on the play, remember? You're starring in Cranford's major musical production tonight!"

Kathy pulled her quilt over her head. "Bad dream," she muttered.

"O.K., you asked for it," said Deena. "I know a surefire way to get you out of bed."

With that announcement Deena began singing at the top of her lungs the title song from *The Sound of Music.*

Kathy sat bolt upright in bed and held up one hand. "Stop!"

Deena shook her head and kept singing until Kathy was completely out of bed and standing groggily in her pajamas on the rug beside her bed. Then she stopped.

"It may not be a great voice," said Deena, "but it's a useful one."

"Hmmmm," Kathy answered as she headed, eyes still closed, for the bathroom.

After a breakfast of buckwheat cakes and bacon, which Kathy hardly dented, the girls went back up to their room to go over the script.

Kathy sat down on her bed, still dotted with the piles Deena had made, and sighed. "I guess Roy and . . . somebody are on their way to the concert by now," she said. "Fifth-row seats! I still can't believe I'm not going!"

"Well," said Deena perkily, "look at the . . . "

"Deena!" cautioned Kathy. "We've been through this!"

"I was only going to say that watching a performance is one thing, but *being* the performance is definitely on a higher level."

Kathy thought about this as she opened her tattered script. "Maybe," she said with a sigh, "you have a point."

Deena flipped through her script, too. "I wish we'd had time last night at rehearsal to go over the final two scenes."

"Everybody's O.K. on those," said Kathy.

Deena shook her head. "I hope what they say about a lousy dress rehearsal meaning a great opening night is true," she said, "because some of the scenes were pretty rough around the edges last night. Hey! Wait a minute! It didn't matter at the beginning of the play that we were short a nun when Lauren took over Lisl's part, but look! Sister Bernice has lines here! In the last scene!"

"Can't one of the other sisters take them?" asked Kathy.

"It won't make sense!" said Deena, shoving the script in front of Kathy's face. "We've got to have another nun!"

"Another nun," repeated Kathy. "I guess maybe you'll have to go on stage after all."

"I guess I will," said Deena. "*If*...the honorable Stewart Sharkey approves."

Suddenly Kathy sprang up from her bed. "Deena!" she shouted. "I've got an even better idea!"

"What?" asked Deena, looking at her cousin suspiciously.

Kathy bent down so that her face was close to Deena's. "You have to promise you'll go along with this," Kathy said. "It would be so great!"

"With what?" asked Deena.

"Just promise!" said Kathy, giggling away.

"O.K., O.K.," said Deena. "I promise."

And with that promise Kathy spelled out her alternate-nun plan to Deena. When she had finished, Deena was shaking her head and laughing, too.

"How did this idea ever occur to you?" Deena asked.

Kathy shrugged. "Who knows? But don't worry. You just have to disappear at the right time."

With their plan worked out, the cousins dug into their script and didn't stop working until nearly six o'clock.

* * *

Kathy sat behind stage and listened to the sounds of the auditorium filling up with the audience that, in about five minutes, would be watching her twirl around singing praises to the hills. Her heart was beating fast. She knew she had the songs down cold. It was the dialogue that worried her. Thank goodness Deena had promised to prompt her from backstage if she needed it.

"I'm counting on you, Kathy." Stewart came up beside Kathy, stone-faced as usual. "This is it. Are you ready?"

Kathy nodded.

"I hope you can do it," he said, shaking his head. "Listen. There's the overture starting. Get on stage."

Kathy gave Stewart a phony little smile. "Yes, sir," she said. Then she smoothed her calf-length nun's dress, adjusted the little gray pinafore she wore over it and stepped onto the stage amid all the cardboard floral arrangements. As the curtain opened, she spread out her arms and began singing with all her heart.

* * *

Before long Kathy was exhilarated with performing, with the audience's wonderful reaction to her songs, and with how well her fellow actors were doing. It seemed such a polished production that she couldn't believe it was the same cast of students that just the night before had been tripping over their own feet and flubbing lines.

The second act began as well as the first. When it was nearly over, Kathy had a short break backstage, just before she and the children began singing at the concert. Now was the time to put her plan into action. She nodded to Deena. Deena nodded back and slipped out of sight.

Kathy hurried over to Stewart, looking frantic.

Stewart saw her look. "What's the matter?"

"It's the last scene, at the convent, when the von Trapps are supposed to be escaping from the Nazis!" whispered Kathy.

"What about it?" asked Stewart.

"There's no nun!" said Kathy. "We've got to have another nun for that scene."

"Oh, my gosh!" said Stewart, madly flipping through his script. "You're right! Where's Deena? She'll have to go on for Sister Bernice."

"I can't find her! And there isn't much time left!" Kathy said. She held up Sister Bernice's long black robe. "Oops! There's my cue, Stewart!" She heaved the habit into Stewart's arms. "I know you'll think of something!" And she entered, stage right.

When Kathy came off stage before the final scene, she saw a frantic Stewart holding Sister Bernice's habit. "I can't find Deena anywhere!" he whispered. "We'll just have to do it without her."

"No! We can't! It won't make sense!" Kathy whispered back. "Think about it!"

"You're right!" wailed Stewart softly. "Where could Deena be?"

Kathy took the habit from Stewart's arms and held it up in front of his body, as if to check the fit. "Looks just about perfect," she said. "And you know what you always say, Stewart, the show must go on!"

Stewart grabbed a script from a nearby chair and mouthed Sister Bernice's lines as he kicked off his loafers and pulled the long black gown over his clothes. "Can you do my headgear?" he asked Kathy.

Kathy quickly fastened the wimple securely around Stewart's chin as Stewart gave her a dagger look. Then, adjusting his expression to reflect inner peace and serenity, he walked gracefully out on stage.

* * *

It was over! The cast was bowing to a wildly clapping audience. Kathy found the finale that Deena and Stewart had invented particularly moving. As the von Trapps climbed the hills into Switzerland—their escape from the Nazis—one by one the other members of the cast joined them in a long line, holding hands and singing "Climb Every Mountain." Then they all took their first bows together. When the audience applauded, the players with minor roles stepped forward, took bows, and left the stage until, at last, just Kathy and Gerard were left. And then, just Kathy. The audience was on its feet exploding with applause for the star of the show. Kathy had to admit, it felt great. Deep down inside she was glad she'd spent four weeks in rehearsal for this, even with all the headaches, instead of joining the Spanish club.

Kathy held out her hands and Stewart, still dressed in his habit, and Deena came on stage to another burst of applause. "Sister Stewart" got a few wolf whistles, which Deena and Kathy loved. Then, before Kathy knew what was happening, flowers were delivered to her and to Deena. Carnations, daisies, and a big bouquet of red roses.

Their arms full of the blossoms and their hearts filled with the joy of success, Deena and Kathy left the stage and the applause died slowly away.

"Can you believe it?" Deena's eyes were brimming with tears.

Kathy shook her head, then looked down at the flowers. "Who are these from?" She sat down on the concrete steps beside the curtain rope backstage, and pulled a card from the carnations. "High score! You were great! Love, Johnny," it said.

"I got one from him, too!" said Deena, leaning over Kathy's shoulder. "That's so sweet."

Ken came up and gave Deena a kiss on the cheek. "You did a great job, Deena," he said.

"Thank you," she replied. "You, too."

"Want to go have a little opening night celebration?" he asked. "Lots of the kids from the cast are going over to the Pizza Hut."

"That sounds great," said Deena.

"These roses are so beautiful! But there's no card," muttered Kathy, turning the large bouquet this way and that, trying to find any small card that might have gotten entangled in the thorns.

"Didn't think they'd need one, Manelli."

Kathy's head jerked up at the sound of that voice.

"Roy!" she screamed, leaping up. "How can you be here?"

Roy shrugged. "I'm here because I'm here." He reached over and pulled Kathy close to him. "And I'm glad I am. You were a world-class Maria."

"Thanks," said Kathy. "But the concert . . ."

"Aw, I handed over the tickets to Ellecia and Zee."

"You mean you *gave* the tickets away?"

Roy shrugged nonchalantly.

"But you could have seen me tomorrow night or next week!" Kathy said, still not believing that Roy was here beside her.

"I wanted to be here tonight," Roy said, and gave her hand a squeeze.

Kathy noticed then that her family was standing around, waiting politely for her to finish talking to Roy. She smiled at them, and Lydia and Nancy rushed forward, catching Kathy and Deena in a big embrace.

"You were both *wonderful!*" said Lydia. "We are the proudest mothers in Cranford!"

"In the U.S.A.!" added Nancy.

"What teamwork!" yelled Johnny, wriggling into their hug. "Can I have your autographs?" he asked. "I think I could sell them to some of the kids in my class for a nickel."

"What a young entrepreneur," said Deena, rubbing Johnny's head.

"He's gonna be a millionaire," added Kathy.

"Why don't you girls get out of your costumes, and we'll go celebrate somewhere," suggested Lydia.

"Time out for Pizza Hut!" cried Johnny as Deena and Kathy headed for the girls' dressing room.

Kathy and Deena wasted no time changing. They hung their costumes on the rack, ready for tomorrow night.

Just as they were giving their hair a quick comb, someone knocked on the dressing room door.

"Come in!" called Deena.

Kathy looked in the mirror and saw a long face peering in the door and then a long woman entering the room.

"Mrs. Dietrich!" she said in surprise, turning in her chair and standing up.

"Kathy!" said Mrs. D., opening her arms to Kathy as if she were a long-lost relative. She gave Kathy a quick embrace. "It's times like tonight that I really congratulate myself," Mrs. Dietrich said to Kathy in a low voice. "In fact, I think I should be made guidance counselor of the year for what I've done with you, Kathy."

Kathy's mouth dropped open and then turned up into a smile. Mrs. D. had a sense of humor!

"Yes," she was going on, in a louder voice now, "when I saw you up on that stage, I thought, Yes, Arlene, you've done the right thing once again! I was awfully proud of myself!" Her eyes were positively twinkling. Kathy couldn't believe it.

Mrs. D. went on. "I have an envelope for you in my desk drawer, Kathy, with some comments I think you'll be proud to take home."

"Oh," said Kathy. "That's great."

Mrs. D. gave Kathy's shoulder a little pat and then turned to Deena. "A very splendid production, Deena," she told her. "I hope we can look forward to more of these from you."

Deena smiled. "I hope so."

"Splendid!" Mrs. Dietrich clapped her long hands together. "Well, I just wanted to congratulate you both." She went out the dressing room door.

Kathy and Deena followed her.

"Hey, Kathy," said Deena as they walked down a backstage passage toward their waiting friends and relatives, "I think this is a first. Looks like you and I are doing something neither of us ever thought we'd do."

"What's that?" asked Kathy.

"Going on a double date!"

"More than double," Kathy laughed. "With a nine-year-old and our mothers as chaperons."

Deena laughed as she took Ken's arm and headed for the stage door. Kathy slipped her hand into Roy's and followed her cousin out into the nippy March air. What a beautiful night, Kathy thought.